RACE FOR THE SPECIES

RACE FOR THE SPECIES

J.L. ALLEN

Archway Publishing books may be ordered through booksellers or by contacting:

Archway Publishing
1663 Liberty Drive
Bloomington, IN 47403
www.archwaypublishing.com
1-(888)-242-5904

ISBN: 978-1-4808-1266-6 (sc)
ISBN: 978-1-4808-1267-3 (e)

Library of Congress Control Number: 2014919084

Printed in the United States of America.

Archway Publishing rev. date: 12/11/2014

FRIDAY DECEMBER 6TH, 5:42 PM.
THE RUSTY ANCHOR SALOON

There wasn't another spot compared to this for miles. Every soldier, sailor, and steamfitter knew it. Pipefitters, journeymen and gypsy cab drivers, huddled together around pool tables, bar stools and bottles of bourbon. Even though the winds are blisteringly coming off of the water, the port is bustling with business. The Wurlitzer churned out yet another Jimmy Buffet tune. The sounds of pool balls and drunken humor reverberated through the lone standing block building. The outside now flooded by blaring yellow crime lights, scoured the surrounding parking lot. It was on the far edge of a busy seaport. No one saw the six astonishing ladies enter the bar. Not seeing them would be as no one observing the big pink elephant in the bouncy house.

Within a few minutes, each of them walked in and made a love connection. By daybreak they were each beginning a five-and-one- half month gestation period. In a six month time, the six women gave birth to six new lives. Six new lives produced-thirty six more that were fully capable, within six months of mating.

A year passes and they can create life and savagely take it as well. The new species now carries DNA and traits both human and what will soon become the new. Each appeared normal, once you got past the fact that they went from infancy to young adult in eight months. They could breathe under water and sustain themselves if protected from the elements at any temperature. They see in total darkness and maneuver at a cruising speed of sixty miles an hour. The laws of gravity did not apply.

CHAPTER I
THE ARRIVAL

Rich, a typical American truck driver, worked average long days for short pay. The Rusty Anchor has been a Friday evening watering hole for Rich and the guys for years. They would meet there after the end of the second shift. After cashing their checks, they swapped stories about this week's weird pickup and delivery. Richard did not say one word about the incident that put him into cardiac arrhythmia. He had no intentions of doing so. As the others gabbed and gulped, he tried unsuccessfully to drown out memories that triggered his original break down.

They asked him on a couple of occasions what caused his collapse. He simply responded 'I don't know, one moment I was waiting on the elevator. The next minute I was on a gurney in an ambulance."

The eight of them together covered all seven quadrants of the city that encircled the port. Adam, the oldest has been with the company since the beginning. It was not clear whether they meant the dawn of time or the start of the corporation. Carl, X-military was a gun enthusiast. He can turn any conversation into a reason to invite everyone out to the rifle range to invoke their second amendment rights.

Eliot, started as package handler a few years back. Denied a dispatch so many times, he called in sick on the last day of the route assignment. Once again, he was passed up for someone with more tenure. He was right, this time his name went uncalled on the new driver roster. Less than a week later an unexpected accident on a fish creek out of town provided him the opportunity he sought for extensively. It gave him the chance to drive all over the city in one of the big brown trucks which helped to show off his legs to secretaries all around the tri-state.

Giovanni, or Gio the Greek, nicknamed for his dark olive complexion and long jet-black ponytail. This image was often the centerpiece of conversation. Both the women and the bosses thought the drivers should have their hair trimmed to no less than an inch above the collar. In the end, it came down to a vote. When the votes are counted, Gio's rank behind the wheel remains secure. So is his name's position at the peak of the bar tab, after he bribed everyone to advocate to let him keep his mane. He always picked up the drink cost on Friday, providing he still had his driving status. Being that he did, the guys ordered top shelf and even offered to pay for Gio's drinks as well.

Then there's Skip. He is named for his uncanny ability to constantly miss a stop anywhere near the farthest point in his route.

Theo, the hustler is known as the brown clown of the downtown rebound.

Next there was Sye. He could not have come off more Jewish if he dresses in black suits or wear a sable beanie full time, with a long white beard and sideburns.

Last of all is Julius. Divorced twice and now married to the shipping business for the sake of monthly child support payments. He is a quiet guy. He'd rather get paid than get laid, the crew often joked. His muscular build is proof of his commitment to strenuous work. If one asks Julius, he is the first to tell you the only thing getting hard is being in debt to the department of children and family services.

The eight men met in the parking lot of The Rusty Anchor every other Friday for the past two years. For seven years, they all walked in together. For seven years, they left with each other. This Friday didn't seem out of the ordinary until the cat calls began.

The rules that stood for years, drowned in Budweiser banter and bullshit. Skip missed another pick up on the third level of his first destination. It meant to go to the eighth floor of the nineteenth and ultimate stop. He didn't notice the mistake until he arrived at the next to last delivery. Then realized, other than the package he was holding in his hand, his truck was currently vacant.

This was usually a good cause for Friday evening jubilation. He knew for a fact that he still had one final shipment scheduled for today. He also knows that his vehicle was now completely empty on the drop-off side. "Then it hit me," skip said, as all hell broke loose. Caterwauling and catcalling jettisoned through the building, from the moment the six of them sauntered through the front door.

The first one entering the lounge was an attractive blond, with skin that looked like polished brass and eyes so sinister they were haunting. The second likewise, stood six feet tall. This one's tress was as raven, as her eyes. The third is pale with bright red hair and a wicked smile. Her eyes are dark and unyielding. The fifth was clothed in white lace and had hair as bleached as cotton. Her pupils appeared silver against the white of her eyes. A deeper look into them would have shown one their own reflection. The final one stood over five and a half feet and was dressed in opaque. Her skin seemed almost translucent. She seemed to practically float above the floor. Her gown is both out of place and out dated for this dank little dock side saloon. The bar is filled with some of the hottest hunks in the shipping business.

Not the guys from UPS, but the Longshoremen, pipefitters and welders who made their living in the boatyards. The pickings would definitely not have been the group of six near the rear of the establishment.

Richard announced that he was going to the men's room to drain the weasel. From Richard's position in front of the urinal he could hear the cheers and jeers. He figured one of the waitresses got a good tip for doing a table top. It's known to happen on a Friday night once the money and the alcohol start flowing full force. He smiled and continued to pee.

Richard returned to find the scene in the pub much different than it had been before going to the bathroom. Besides a couple of drunks, one was at the far corner of the bar, unconscious. The other, slouched on a chair at the other side of the men's room. Their table was empty. Rich thought the patrons and employees had scurried outside to witness one of the drunken rumbles that break out from time to time. He then sauntered out into the early evening, as several others began to make their way back inside. "Who won?" Rich asked, not really expecting a reply. "Those guys," answered a burly boatyard worker, pointing over his shoulder toward the parking lot.

Following his lead and apparently the rest of the packed bar's, Richard walked out into the pavement and headed to where they had all parked. Richard noticed instantly the empty spaces where his friend's vehicles had been only moments ago. Everyone else was now making their way back into the bar, several of them guffawing, that it was the damnedest thing they had ever seen.

He did not want to believe that each and every one of them left him, in the short time that it took him to take a whiz. Richard pulled out his cellular and called Gio. He had Gio's number the longest. At least two of the other guys cell phone numbers as well.

There was no luck reaching Gio. He received same response dialing Carl's digits, then Adam's. With each he got the reply, "I'm sorry, but the person you're trying to reach traveled out of the calling area. Can you please try your call again later?" After a few minutes Richard strolled into the building. Everything returned to normal and other people occupied their table. He walked over to the waitress at the bar. "What just happened?" he inquired. She looked at him as if she has never seen him before. Proceeding to ask, "What are you drinking handsome?" He mumbled something incoherent, turned and treaded back out to the big parking lot.

He stood mystified, near the rear of his car. He glanced over to where a few moments earlier, his friend's vehicles were positioned. Other patrons coming to the bar now filled the spaces. No one seemed to remember that just a few short minutes ago, seven guys in brown shorts, were enjoying drinks at the Anchor. Richard jumped into his own vehicle, backed out, and made a beeline for the highway.

Nothing made any sense at the moment and Rich realized quickly that he was once again on the edge of passing out. He knew this more from his training than instinct. He pulled over onto the shoulder and put his car in park. As Rich sat trying hard to digest the last half hour's events, he could feel his chest heaving. He Attempted to breathe, and he was sure that he was about to go into shock, yet again.

In a full panic, he dialed 911 and placed his cellular on speaker before dropping it into the passenger seat. "9-1-1 do you have an emergency?" A female's voice crackled from the speakers over Rich's cell phone. "Yes, I'd like to make a missing person's report, I think," Richard said, sounding almost hysterical to the calm operator on the other end. "What's the age and gender of the person you would like to report missing sir?" the woman asked calmly. But Richard's mind raced with the consequences of following through on this call and he stopped talking, reached over, and pressed the button to disconnect the call. He rested for more than a few minutes, trying to catch his breath when he heard the familiar sound of a police car in his proximity.

Rich fought the urge to panic, forcing each and every gulp of air to the surface, as he sat waiting for the officer to approach. After what seemed to Richard like forever, the deputy finally approached his vehicle from the passenger side rear. After assessing the situation, he tilted down and looked in the back of the car. He continues toward the front where Rich was in an almost catatonic state in the driver's seat. "Sir, are you having a medical emergency?' he asked, as he leaned in and opened the door, using the inside handle.

Richard could only shake his head yes. The officer bends in close and examines his pulse, and then checks the dilation of his pupils with a small penlight attached to his shirt.

The police man yelled a bunch of call numbers into a radio adhered to an epilate on his shoulder. Then he climbed into the car with Richard, undoing his seat belt. He tried desperately to distract him from the passenger side of the vehicle so that he could lay him down and get a clear airway. The officer thought for sure that Rich was having a heart attack. The cop worked feverishly to pull him out of his car and onto his back on the ground next to it.

It wasn't until the cop leaned in close to undo the first couple of buttons on Richard's shirt when he smelled the faint odor of alcohol.

It was at this point that the police man had gone from friendly community servant to an officer sworn to protect the world from drunk drivers.

"How much have you had to drink this evening?" the cop asked Richard condescendingly. He did not even wait for his response as he reached to the back of his utility belt and disengaged the silver cuffs hanging there. "At this point Sir I need to inform you that after detecting the faint odor of alcohol on your breath and finding you behind the wheel of a motor vehicle, I must advise you that you have the right to remain silent and anything you say can and will be used against you in a court of law."

SATURDAY DECEMBER 7TH 12:03 PM

Six experienced divers, obtaining photos of the establishment of a new reef system, formed in the South Florida coast line, are missing this afternoon about five miles off of the Hollywood seashore. While taking pictures to check for the development of any current growth to the retired navy destroyer, used as target practice in war games a couple of years back, have simply vanished. A gentleman known only as Darryl, from Ft. Lauderdale has a fishing boat named The Sea Dragon. Their vessel came upon a boat about nine miles southeast as they left to go out on their first run. They thought little of the empty ship, since several dive flags were in the water.

It wasn't until they were returning from just under three hours of no fish and found the craft still berthed in the exact same place. It prompted the ship's commander to contact the coast guard to report a possible issue. The crew of the Dragon fishing boat anchored about a hundred yards out and waited on the rescuers to arrive. While at the anchor the boat's Captain gave the go ahead to let their patrons fish, since that is after all what they were paid to do. "I've never seen anything like it," said the admiral.

"From that second the first hook hit the water; they were reeling in Red Snapper and Spanish mackerel to blues and striped bass. Every one of our wells are filled to the hilt with everything from baby octopus to up to sixty pound groupers."

"For the first time in my memory, hell my life even, we actually had to quit because there was nowhere else to put the fish. I'm pretty sure we've exceeded the dragon's weight capacity. In fact the only thing I haven't seen them pull out of here this morning was Jellyfish, sea otter and those missing divers," he said. The captain took his hat off and placed it over his heart. He then turned in the direction of the empty vessel.

What's bad is there are nevertheless six experienced dive photographers whose whereabouts are as yet still unknown. Although no one has officially used the term lost at sea. On a good note, The Sea Dragon's fishing boat tours are now booked for the remainder of the month of December.

At the moment of broadcast, the rescuers were still unsuccessful at finding out the names of the missing persons, or at contacting any of the involved next of kin.

Not until Coast Guard divers went down for the fifth time, was the order finally given for Sea-Tow to secure the vessel and pull it to Broward Sheriff's Office Marine Lab.

As the 4-man crew made its way to the shore with the ill faded barge, the Sea Dragon headed northwest toward the Ft. Lauderdale water front.

Later, after many failed attempts to contact the boat by radio, other fishing boats were contacted to see if anyone had a visual on the large craft. It seemed that no one had seen or heard from it since The Sea-Tow left with the deserted dive vessel. The 10-man crew with its eight male passengers has seemingly vanished.

A second call to the coast guard in a matter of hours didn't quite give them information that could help. It told them more than they wanted to know. Word from the rescue Station at Port Everglades, Ft. Lauderdale, said the Coast Guard Cutter Lawrence had been called out to assist in the search for the six divers. He never returned to base, less than four nautical miles from where the missing boat had been sighted. When the Sheriff's Department was informed of this, they too realized that the sixteen foot Dusky Marine with its crew of 2 men and The Sea Tow with 4 sailors, and the dive vessel, have now disappeared.

The Coast Guard and a crew of twenty four sailors are missing, along with eighteen men from the Dragon fishing boat, the assemblage of the Sea Tow vessel and the two Marine Life officers on the Dusky. Forty-eight disappeared, whereas a few hours earlier there had been only six.

Had anyone thought to add up the disappearances around south Florida alone on this tropical winter afternoon, their discovery might have been startling. The total count of men missing in the area rose to forty-eight. The total amount across the state was four hundred twenty. Across the nation, thirty-six hundred eighteen, and around the world, just over two point four million men vanished in a day. It was before 9 AM when an officer came to the cell to retrieve Rich for his appearance before the Magistrate.

Richard is introduced to a young man that looked fresh out of High School, wearing a very expensive suit, carrying a file and a brief case. "I'm here as your public defender," said the young man. Richard and the court appointed attorney shook hands briefly, and the lawyer asked only one question. "How many drinks did you have at The Rusty Anchor last night Mr. Ruskin?" Rich reflected briefly before answering, "Only one, we had just arrived, saw some people leaving from a table near the rear, and made a B-line for the slab. Then we ordered our beverage from a server, and I remember telling the guys, if I'm going to drink beer I'm going to have to unload some of this still warm coffee."

Richard grinned skittishly, as the young public defender, now frantically shuffling through papers in his file, retrieved one of a few hand written documents from the parsonage of paperwork. He held it so close to his own face that Richard thought for a moment he might be attempting to look through the document instead of at it.

"In saying we Mr. Ruskin you're referring too?" He looked at Rich, totally anticipating him completing his sentence. "The guys I work with" he said with a slight heir of aggravation; "Adam, Carl, Skip, Gio, Theo and Sye." "Would that be Adam Gray, Carl McNeal, Danny Skip turner, Giovanni Pirelli, Theodore Grimsby and Sidney Greenburg?" the counsellor asked Richard as if he were reading the paper in front of him through some kind of third eye on his forehead. Richard almost laughed, in spite of his situation, a laugh that was all but frozen in the moment when the lawyer spoke again. "And where are the men now?" inquired the young public defender.

With a stern face and chiseled chin that made him look more like a cartoon character than an attorney. "Well it is Saturday. Our routes run a little different on the weekends, so I couldn't tell you where each of them would be in the city right now. We kept in contact by cell phones, supplied by our company, for several reasons, safety being only one of them."

He seemed to gaze at Rich the same way he seemed to stare through the piece of paper with the hand written notes all over it. The young man then looked directly into Richards eyes and asked, "Do you have any idea why neither of those guys have been seen or heard of since?" I mean six men with stellar performance records, seven when I include you, but you're here Richard. Your six co-workers just vanished off the face of the earth." Richard, having learned this for the first time, suddenly felt faint. He thought back on the last moment he spotted Adam, speeding past him in his prized 57 Chevy, his grin sealed in a florescent glow, supposedly from the car's radio.

"What is working in your favor is, the fact that there was never a breathalyzer or any other test ever taken to prove you were driving impaired."

"Two, the fact you were not driving, even though you're a legal licensed driver, behind the wheel of an automobile. Your vehicle was parked when the officer came upon you. Those charges will undoubtedly be dropped today."

Richard smiled graciously as soon as he had heard this, a smile that was again instantaneously destroyed by the young attorney's next words. "Now, for the matter of the federal Investigation" the attorney said. "Federal investigation? what federal investigation?" Richard yelled in the small holding area. "What the hell is going on?" Rich said with a look of total disbelief. "That's exactly what everyone wants to know as well Mr. Ruskin. I've been assigned by this county to represent you in this matter. Other than getting public intoxication and drunken charges dismissed there's very little else I can do." "But how the hell did this go from a possible DUI to a dam federal investigation?" Richard almost screamed in question as he stepped close enough to the young lawyer for several bailiffs to take notice.

The young attorney, who seemed unperturbed in the least, simply took a step back and then looked straight into Richards eyes. "There are six men missing Mr. Ruskin, and it seems you are the last person either of them contacted." When Rich is finally released on his own recognizance, he is directed to a desk. There, he was asked to sign the form attached to a clipboard before he would be allowed to reclaim his personal effects. The first thing he saw when he opened the large envelope was his company cellphone.

A lump instantaneously filled his throat, causing Richard to swallow without thinking. His wallet, his web belt, a couple of pens and markers, and some loose change, were the only things in the bag. "My keys, where are my keys?" Rich asked. "Probably where ever your vehicle is Sir, I'm not the arresting officer. I'm just here to make sure that your leaving here goes as expeditiously as possible." To Richard the cop seemed overly anxious, as he signed the sheet, pocketing all of his smaller items, for the time being, into one pocket. He then picked up the release forms and looked at them dumbfounded before handing them across the counter to the nervous official and inquired, "How do I find out where my car is?" Rich questioned, now sounding a little impatient. The policeman pushed the reading glasses up off of the tip of his nose and scanned the top corners of the paper quickly before replying; "If you've got a DUI pending I wouldn't recommend you do that but . . ."

"I don't have a DUI, Rich shot back, I wasn't found guilty, can you just tell me where the hell they would have towed my car too?" The now slightly irritated officer grabbed a slip off of the table that had a picture of a police tow truck on it. He shoved it across the counter at Richard. "The tow yards address is on the other side of that card. Go out that door, turn left, and go around the building and down two blocks to the double gates on the left side of the street. Ring the buzzer underneath the sign and wait for the intercom to give you further instructions.

Then follow them to the letter," the cop said, holding his arm up and pointed toward the exit a little too long for Richard's liking. He spoke in a monotone that would have probably caused Richard to crack had he not been only a couple of yards from freedom.

After scooping up his belt and folding his release paper into his left breast pocket, Rich gave one final glance at the antsy cop before walking quickly out the door and into the Saturday sun.

Rich all but ran to the impound lot, where he did exactly as the officer had told him, pressed the buzzer beneath the sign and waited. The Intercom crackled noisily before a female voice with a tinny tone asked, "How can I help you?" "Hi, my car was towed and I was sent here to pick it up," Richard said. "Give me the number on your release form Sir; that will be the digits in the box with the highlighter mark over it," she stated, sounding as if she were chewing bubblegum between each word.

Frustrated yet resigned to the fact, rich turned and walked back the two and a half blocks to City Hall, Richard made his way back to the center of town and the huge City Hall Complex. The ATM machine sat in the far corner of the lobby in a sunken waiting area. Before stepping down the two steps to where the ATM machine sat, Rich waited up top, so as not to spook a pretty young lady currently in the lobby.

Then Richard read the number off to her and waited patiently for a buzzer to signal, that a gate was about to open. "That will be two-hundred eighty-six dollars cash Sir" The lady said in a tiny voice. "Are you shitting me? Two hundred eighty-six, cash? I got a credit card." "Then you also have a problem" the woman squawked. "There's an ATM in the lobby of the police station, but we don't take cards Sir. Cash only."

A lady was in the middle of her own transaction at the ATM machine. Richard decided to use this time to try contacting his job and attempt to somehow explain his absence. After pulling the cell out from underneath the bundle of pens and markers in his vest, Rich pressed the power button, only to find the phone was already on. It showed a low battery warning, and then signed right back off again.

"Dam it," he said under his breath as he now shoved the phone into his left breast pocket. The woman finished her business and walked toward Rich. For the first time he got a full view of her and found himself instantly aroused by her beauty. Her skin had a glow he has never seen before, and her eyes were like pools of green . . . and then she was gone.

The beautiful young woman had apparently either miss judged the steps, or just missed them all together, and tumbled to her knees, right at Richard's feet. Richard immediately swooped down to one knee to offer her assistance. His strong hands grasped her tenderly about her shoulders. In an instant Rich felt an arousal that he had not noticed since finding his dad's girly magazines, hidden in between his parent's mattress and box spring.

Their eyes met briefly, which was long enough to make Richard desire her like he hadn't desired a woman in all of his adult life. He helped her to her feet, and she mumbled something totally inaudible to him, before scurrying up the two steps and around the corner and out of view. It wasn't until that moment that he spotted the small bulge in the center of a perfectly formed female body.

Rich wanted badly to run after her, but was torn between his desires to know her and his need to use the ATM, to get both his car and his job out of impound. He was then faced with the reality that he'd best stick to the game plan. She is beautiful, and apparently in a relationship, he figured because she appeared to be just a little bit pregnant. Richard pulled his debit card from his wallet, quickly made his transaction, pocketed his cash and headed out the way he came in.

As he walked back out into the daylight, Rich still hoped that the young lady might have been waiting outside, perhaps for a cab or a bus. Much to his chagrin, the woman was nowhere in sight.

Even Richard found himself overwhelmed because the thought of her has taken over his mind. It made it hard to concentrate on what it was he so badly needed to get done as quickly as was humanly possible. He reached the gate of the impound lot, rang the bell and communicated his intentions to the tiny voice on the intercom.

He announced that he has cash and needs into the compound to reclaim his car and advance his way to the shipping complex. Rich is currently more than eleven hours late for work. As soon as he arrived, he caught a beeline straight for his boss's office. Stares from coworkers that have seen him every day for years, directly glared at him as if they were now seeing an aberration. Richard knocked on the door to the room and then entered to find it unoccupied. He considered waiting there for him but, a chaotic bellow from the conference room down the hall let Rich know his Boss's exact whereabouts.

Richard stepped into the conference room and instantly the chaos became a momentary total silence. His boss stared at him, mouth open, chin dropped, as if both air and thought had been swept from him in a split second. "Is this some kind of a joke," Rich's boss said to him, after seeming to finally regain his ability to both breathe and to speak.

"Because if this is some kind of a God damned joke," his boss bellowed. "You'd best be here dropping off the keys and the phone. I'll see to it that you and neither one of the other men can get a reference to drive a garbage truck after this. You got any idea how much your guys little prank has caused this company today alone? And where the hell are those other four ass holes anyway, because I swear I'm ready to rip each one of you a new ass hole."

"We all met up at The Anchor, last night after work, around six or just a little after" Richard started. "After getting a table and ordering drinks, I retrieved my beer and went to the men's room. I returned and thought there had been a brawl or something in the parking area. When I came back in a matter of a few minutes, I found the bar literally deserted." "So where in hell are the other guys?" his boss roared." "I don't know" Rich replied almost unintelligibly, "I did walk out to the lot in time to see Adam Gray drive by, headed toward the exit. I tried contacting each of them on their cell phones. Each moment I called, I got a message saying that they had traveled out of their calling zone." "That's bullshit!" his manager all but growled, "Those dam Motorola's are good for up to two hundred miles from home base. What kind of hogwash you selling me?"

Richard felt defeated; "And where's your phone now?" his boss asked him with a snarl. Rich reached into his brown uniform shirt's left breast pocket, pulled out the Motorola and held it out in front of him. As if to show his manager that he still had it.

"Try dialing them now!" his manager barked. With his head down like a scorned child, Richard mumbled, "it's dead Sir." "More bullshit" the director proclaimed as he retrieved his own cellular from his pocket and dialed. "I'm sorry, but the person you're trying to reach has apparently traveled outside of the calling area, can you please try your call again later." His boss hung up and dialed Gio's number next. He received the same reply then hung up and dialed each of the other guy's cell phones and with each he got the exact same message. "How on earth is this possible and what in hell is going on here" Richard's boss bellowed questioningly. Rich had no answer and wisely give no response.

"Listen, I don't know what in tar-nations is going on, but I do intend to get to the bottom of it," his boss said gruffly. "And I tell you this, if I find out that this was a crank, I'll eat through your asses like a sub sandwich, you get my drift?" Richard again bowed his head like a scorned kid before nodding that he understood. "I'm too short handed to fire you at the moment. I've already sent someone else out on your route, what other choice did I have? seven guys stiffed me, all on the same damned day. Stop in personnel and switch out that blasted phone" said the manager. "If your ass ain't here Monday morning when those front gates open you're done."

Rich bowed his head and nodded once more before turning on his heels and heading back out into the hallway. Instead of pivoting left to return out to the parking area, Richard turned right, proceeding deeper into the building. After strolling only a few yards, he came to a doorway sign that stated employees only, pushed it open and walked in. On the other side of the door was a line of lockers, affronted by a row of benches. This is where he and the men had spent countless hours exchanging jokes and wise cracks. The employee lounge now felt ominously empty. He then ambled first to his own locker, then went over and touched each of the guy's lockers compassionately before walking out of the room. After climbing behind the wheel of his car, Rich secured his seat belt and started out of the lot. As he drove past the forefront entrance where Human Resources was located, he couldn't help but notice a very pretty young woman entering the front of the structure.

Besides he could not help but notice that although she looked strikingly beautiful, she'd also seemed more than a little pregnant. A dozen men from the fishing trawler "Sea Nemesis" are missing. They are now presumed lost in the ocean, after leaving Alice Town Bimini, in the Bahamas sometime after four AM Saturday morning. It appeared they headed due west toward Miami, to do some angling in the Florida straits, off of the coast. Departing before the day, with calm seas, and heading into storm free waters, many claim that The Devil's Triangle has simply claimed another boat load of victims. This will make the twelve males sort of folk heroes back around the Bimini boatyards.

On The Virginia side of the Potomac River, precisely outside the gates of Dahlgren Naval Warfare Systems, a group of guys on leave were roughhousing in the water. They were exactly south of Crain

Highway and the 301 Harry W Nice Memorial bridge. They had left their cellphones and other belongings lying on their towels, about thirty feet from the shoreline at just past 3PM.

It was approximately after 5PM and just after dusk when a Resource Official, securing the sector for the night, came across the items on the beach and called it in. In no time the region was flooded with flashlights along the shore. Marine patrol boats on the water from the base, Maryland and Virginia State Police combed the shorelines. Searching through Chapel Point State Park to the north, to Point Lookout in the south where the mouth of the Potomac opened up to the Chesapeake. A couple of guys pulling up traps between Piney point Creek & Herring Creek were asked if they'd seen anything out of the ordinary in the area. They simply responded by pointing at the back of their small crab vessel. Every space that could hold a crab was now stuffed with both crab and catfish. The crab pot they had managed to pull up without breaking the strings had been packed to the verge of bulging. Each filled and bursting with catfish and crab, trying desperately to devour each other.

Meanwhile back on the beach at naval Support Facility, the identity of the persons owning the abandoned items were coming in over the Navy shortwave radio. All six of them, stationed just a few hundred yards of their current position, at Dahlgren's weapons laboratory, are now missing. A full fledge exploration included US Navy divers and mini submersibles with dual lighting and sonar equipment. All next of kin had been notified and shortly after midnight, the search was called off. The guys seemingly vanished in midair. It wasn't until the local community learned about the incident via the morning news that a couple finally came forward. The two stated that they had actually seen six adult male with crew cuts, hanging out on the Virginia side of the Potomac River. "We saw them about quarter mile south of the Harry Nice Bridge. They'd been out boating all day and returning from Solomon's Island when we noticed a dozen men horse playing along the water's edge." "It looked as if they were playing Frisbee football," the man said. "They ran darting and dodging all along the water's edge," the woman continued, but . . . "They were not alone."

The couple made note that it would have had to have been right around four thirty. It gets dark by five, and they were already moored in their backyard in Pomonkey when evening arrived. The wife also mentioned that the tide started emerging, not going out. She remembered because when the tide approaches in on their private sea wall, all the tall sea grass tend to pile up along the walls edge. It's a pain in the ass, as she puts it, when trying to tie off. "The current was definitely advancing" both said simultaneously to a WJLA News reporter. "So if the water flow is coming in then the search should be proceeding north toward DC don't you think?" the man's wife asked; now more to get her face on TV than out of curiosity.

"What can you tell me about what you saw before passing under the Harry Nice Bridge?" the reporter asked almost anxiously. The two of them tried successfully to suck up air time. The wife was the first to jump in front of the camera, but her husband was already spitting all over the mic. "We just got back from a day of funning and sunning over at Solomon's. And I consistently slow down quite a bit coming through here, because of the public beach area. No wake zone and all you know," he stated. "I noticed them right away," she jumped in, the crew cuts, the muscularity. I kind of figured them to be either military or police or both. After all they were southwest of the Harry Nice, the coastline is basically on the North West side," she said. "Of course she would spot them. She always had an eye for burliness," he uttered, pretending not to observe that he was now flexing whatever chest muscles he still had left.

"He might have seen em first had it not been for the shit load of Hoochies walking half naked along the water's edge," the wife stated, with a smirk that resembled a jealous school girl. "Hoochies?" the newsman asked. She quickly snatched the microphone from in front of her husband's lips, jamming it in front of hers. "Yeah, Hoochie Mommas is what I call em, with their lil flimsy string bikinis on. Strolling around, throwing their ass everywhere like they're trying to throw their backs out of whack or something." "Did you get a good look at them? Notice any unique characteristics?" the journalist questioned again.

"Well I'm sure if they possessed a tattoo or even a birthmark this one would have spotted it" she said, shoving an expensively manicured thumb in her husband's direction. "Hell I had to grab the wheel to keep us from running into the damned bridge pylon," his wife blurted out excitedly. The reporter pushed the mic back toward the husband, who was more than happy to take it. "Each of em had legs to die for" he said. "You still might," the wife added, as he prepared his hands to help him describe the shapeliness of the women in question. "There were six of ladies' and all tall and gorgeous, stunning even. Tanned everywhere and all if you know what I'm trying to say," he continued. "There was one that stood out though. She was the only woman I got a good face to face look at. She appeared foreign, like from some other country and she walked with a slight limp. I automatically figured she'd been involved in some type of accident or something, because she had a cleft lip, right down the middle. I mean her mouth seemed almost as if it had been split like a fish," he went on saying, looking totally serious at this point. "You mean a cleft palette, don't you?" the reporter replied back curiously. "Hell no!" the husband repeated, "This chick's lips looked as if they had been put on vertically.

By the morning, Fox news spread it all across the country. Six high ranking U S Military officials were now missing and assumed kidnapped from Dahlgren Virginia's from Aegis Training and readiness center Dahlgren Naval Warfare Systems.

The six men, whose identities have been withheld, were stationed at the training center. Last seen along the Virginia side of the Potomac River, south of the Harry Nice Bridge that connects Virginia to Maryland. A witness told reporters he and his wife were on their way home from Solomon's Island. Just off of the overpass they saw the sailors frolicking near the shoreline with six women. One whose face, he reported to WJLA News, shaped almost like a fish. WSVN 7 News in Ft. Lauderdale announced that a passing boater said the guys, have been spotted by the water's edge with ladies that looked as if they were mermaids. Before long, each hotel and motel beside the 301 corridor, from Brandywine Maryland in the north, to Fort A P Hill in Virginia north of Richmond's I-95 was completely filled. Every TV satellite truck in the eastern hemisphere seems to converged on Southern Maryland and North Eastern Virginia in the days to follow.

Every Cafe, Diner, and Dunkin Doughnuts are filled to the gills, for lack of a better term, and abuzz with everything from reporters, photographers, and photojournalist, to trappers and treasure hunters. The Potomac River was now plastered with powerboats; both the Maryland and Virginia shorelines were packed with marine patrols with metal detectors to boy scouts with bags and nets.

As for tourism, the entire fiasco resulted in an economic resurgence that should have been both talked about and felt for years. Every waterfront street from Port Tobacco to Pomonkey Maryland had its own TV news crew. Police and marine patrol officers tried unsuccessfully, to cordon the area, due to the fact that it was mostly public access. A lot of it was waterfront parks and camping. Not only the locals, but massive mobile homes from as far away as Montana had already shown up on thinly graveled roads. The small yet historical, tobacco farms of Southern Maryland had presently become a part of the breakdown of mankind as we now know it. Each boat slip between Belle Haven Country Club on the northwest shore of the Potomac River, just south of the Washington DC line and the Woodrow Wilson Bridge, had a vessel moored to it, whether legally or illegally. People crowded the waters in anything that would float. Residents flooded the beaches with partiers and others with poor perception of the depth of the problem at hand. Later that evening, in Bel Alton Maryland, north of where the sailors had gone missing, two hundred bickers, from all along the eastern corridor, descended on Ape Hangers Saloon, Known to the locals as a shit kicking biker bar.

That evening eighty or so local bikers, joined by over two hundred outsiders, were now becoming as drunk and belligerent as they themselves had been for years. Three hundred and nine bikers brawled that night, eighty-six of them were apprehended, and eighteen were never seen again. Outside of Ape Hangers, the next morning, eighteen chrome machines sat unclaimed, the owners assumed arrested.

The following few days appeared to be business as usual all over the world. Despite the fact that just over three and a half million men had disappeared worldwide in the past week. Airports and train stations managed to maintain their schedules. Until one pilot from each major airport along the east coast ended up with full, scheduled flights and missing pilots or co-pilots. Six male navigators, with stellar performance records, seemed to have vanished in thin air.

What was even stranger was that each pilot or co-pilot had actually reported to their assigned airports. Some, as a matter of fact had been seen by other members of their own flight crew, in the airport and in route to their flights.

Michael Troupe was typically used to being up at 3 AM. He was more accustomed to sleeping in first class than he was to the new queen sized double pillow top mattress that he has at home.

He had done the Atlanta to Dallas-Fort Worth flight so many times at 6:15 in the morning that he'd actually gotten physically ill during his two week vacation. Now, as he exited the cab and entered the concourse, briefcase in hand, uniform immaculately pressed, Captain Troupe Looked like a television commercial add, as he passed through the crowded airport. He was molested by the eyes of quite a few lonely women and more than enough men. He made his way across toward the private, employee only section of the airport. He stopped to relieve himself in a men's bathroom outside of the Commodore's Lounge. Then he saw a beautiful young woman stumble from the ladies room, falling almost as if scripted, into his waiting arms. From the green tint to her skin he concluded that she was just off of an overseas flight. Apparently nauseated, even in this present state, Michael couldn't help but notice that she manifested the deepest hazel eyes he had ever had the pleasure of staring into.

Their stares locked momentarily before Michael was filled with an overwhelming urge to brush his lips against this stranger with the alluring green eyes. The look that stared back at him told him she longed for a kiss as badly as he.

So he leaned in, their lips met, and she sucked in deeply. She liquefied him completely, instantly drinking him in, like one of those squirting fountains, in the park, in summer; the ones that shot streams of water from many holes, simultaneously, only in reverse.

Michael was condensed and devoured, before the next travel weary couple rounded the corner to enter the restrooms. They politely stepped around the strangely dressed woman, kneeling on the tile floor just outside of the ladies room. When they returned from their perspective bathrooms, the young lady was gone. So they kind of figured she'd either been praying that she'd have a secured trip out or because she'd had a safe flight in. Either way, neither gave it any more thought. They strolled back toward their gate, in time for the pretty middle aged blond to announce they would begin boarding passengers sitting in the tail of the airplane. Since the two had requested rear seats, this meant them. They were in the perfect position to wait on the plane for almost a couple of hours while authorities searched the airport for their now missing pilot. The female then walked into the bathroom unobserved, slipped into the farthest stall and flushed.

In New York's LaGuardia Airport, 1st Officer Keith Owens, referred to by friends as chocolate muscles, was being his normal flirtatious self. Then he looked upon a very pregnant looking woman going into an elevator. Even though the lady didn't appear to have any luggage, the pilot saw this as another opportunity to show off his manly charms and boyish good looks.

The elevator door had almost closed completely when he reached it, but Keith managed to get a couple of fingers between the slats, tripping the sensor. As it reopened a mannish charmed man walked in. The woman seemed at this moment, below that point of what he and his colleagues had called too pregnant to fly.

"Thank you for stopping the elevator for me beautiful," Keith started to say, just as the doorway began to close. The elevator rose to the next level, the expecting female, stumbled out, holding the handrails with one hand and her under belly with the other. The hooded, coat like contraption that she wore appeared to be stretching at the seams as she made her way along the wall to a well. Partially leaning, partly stooped, she knelt over the sprout, using the panel behind it to balance herself. The lady pressed the button on the side of the fountain and the water flowed upward to her lips.

As she appeared to drink, anyone watching, had there been, would have noticed the stress in her garb ease. The hem of her covering now went from below her calves to just above, dragging the floor. As she stood, straightening her disheveled attire, the woman seemed to have an almost youthful glow. She turns and walks back toward the elevator, her roughly anorexic frame hidden under her bulky cover of clothing.

As she moved toward the elevator, a burly businessman reached out and pressed the button for her, which allowed her frail, almost fang like fingers to remain hidden under her clothing. When the elevator opened next at the lower floor, the full figured female stepped out of the elevator alone and walked hastily across the vastness of the airport's luggage pick up area and out the front door.

Within seconds the button to access the elevator was pushed again, this time by a woman traveling with her toddler of about two years old. In a hurry to get to their designated boarding zone, the lady paid no attention at all to the small puddle of clear sticky liquid, with the pinkish nucleus. Holding her young son in what she called a mother's very protective grip. The lift again rose to the following level. The mom ruffled her son's hair. Then knelt down on one knee to adjust his collar and wipe the sleep from his little eyes. The ding of the bell alerted her to their arrival on the upper level. She rose, again took her young son's hand, and proceeded into the upper concourse. Nothing had alerted them to the fact that the sticky liquid somehow managed to slide across the level elevator floor on its own. It attached itself to the bottom of her toddler's right shoe, soaking his sock by the time they cleared the lift. The boy's entire body shuddered momentarily, his palm seeming to spasm briefly in his mother's hands. "Are you OK little buddy?" she asked giddily, "did you catch a slight chill baby boy?"

A young girl on winter break from high school in Boston, where she was in her sophomore year, was on her way to the mid-west with her parents. They planned six months for a ski trip in the Colorado Rockies.

After being advised by air terminal security that she couldn't take her favorite water bottle into the airport, and at the promise from her parents that they'd replace it at the nearest store, she reluctantly tossed the partially full plastic of spring water into a nearby trash receptacle. The girl's parents kept their commitment, buying her a jumbo jug in the very first gift shop they came across.

She quickly ripped the tag off, waited patiently behind a lady wearing too many coats and filled it before their flight. Her mom and dad continued to walk, slowly ahead, while she topped it up almost to the rim. Closing the bottle top tightly, the teen took a long sip of the icy cold liquid from the straw. She embedded it through the center of the cap of her new, dark green juice flask, before running to join them, walking steadily in front of her in the concourse.

The flight to Denver International was uneventful. She'd actually slept until the plane came down. Her parents, not being seasoned travelers, simply took it as jet lag. As they rose to exit the aircraft, she reached over and picked up the now half empty water bottle. She thought to herself that the jug felt heavier than it had when it had been totally full. The girl quickly brushed this off as being a result of the altitude here in Colorado. After all it was the mile high city and everyone knew that weights varied in higher altitudes, right?

By the time the trio caught the underground train from where they landed, to where they needed to pick up their luggage, she noticed she drank over half of the water in the bottle. By the time her parents rented a minivan and stuffed it with their luggage, she was more than glad to just climb into the rear seat and go back to sleep for their almost two hour drive from the airport to their resort hotel in Estes Park Colorado.

Her mother hinted that they all stop and eat somewhere, to sample the local fare, as she'd put it, but the teen suddenly felt bloated and a little nauseous. "Why don't we just hit a drive through and get on to where we need to go," she suggested. Her father agreed, and the Mom went along with the two of them. But within minutes of eating a small garden salad and finishing her bottled water, the young girl doubled over in pain and lay back in the car. Her scream startled her mom so badly that she quickly unbuckled her seat belt and made a mad dash to join her daughter on the rear seat of the minivan. What the mother saw when she reached the back seat scared her so that she herself screamed, before dropping to her knees beside her fifteen-year-old teenager. She placed the back of her hand against her daughter's forehead and immediately yelled for her husband to run them to a hospital. The adolescent was grabbing her stomach because it ached, trembling from chills and soaked with sweat from a massive fever.

The GPS said that there was a hospital in Bloomfield, only moments away and her father got them there within a matter of minutes. Her mom called ahead and had a crisis team waiting at the emergency entrance when they arrived. The trip to the ER was totally unexpected, so was the doctor's final diagnosis. Their fifteen year old daughter was nearly nine months pregnant, and seemed to be going into labor at this very minute.

"How long have you been sexually active?" The nurse asked the girl calmly. "I've Never," she cried. "My baby can't be expecting, she just cheered their high school football team on to a state championship last week. She was top of the pyramid, what do you mean she's pregnant? We just flew out here to go skiing in the mountains, that can't be possible," the mother declared to the doctor. The MD quickly stopped the gurney as it passed, pulled back the blankets now covering the young girl on it, in route to the operating room.

"How could you not have known?" The doctor asked, as he and her parents got a good view at the girl's now massively stretched, badly bulging body. The mother fainted instantly into the father's arms. With help from the attending medical personnel, the father was able to assist them in laying his wife out flat on the floor. He himself then lost consciousness, collapsing over top of her. A surgical team rushed the girl down the hall, while ER staff concentrated on reviving her parents.

The physician on duty thought this nothing more than another instance of a teen who has lied to her parent's about her pregnancy, covering it up until the last possible moment. It wasn't until the doctor took a close look between the young lady's legs on the delivery table that the case took an even stranger turn. The young woman's hymen was yet totally intact. The MD immediately ordered a sonogram, which scared him more than her still attached and sealed hymen. The baby inside of her was not only ready to come out, but showed signs of already having teeth and appeared to be trying to chew its way out.

Jay Striker had been the fly by the seat of your pants type of guy ever since childhood. Now that Jay had earned a position as co-pilot for a major airlines, he made a promise to play it straight. He had given himself more than enough time to reach New York's, LaGuardia airport, regardless of the fact that there was a slow steady rainfall and people in the area. They really did not drive well in good weather, none the less in incumbent weather. He drove the rental car more than a few miles an hour under the speed limit, until he came upon a convertible sports coup, sitting on the edge of the airport's perimeter road. A woman in the driver seat had the top down, in the pouring rain.

Jay did think, "Why the hell is she just sitting there with the top down? Why does she not at least try to put it up manually?" It never crossed his mind to stop and get out in the pouring rain to go help this woman out. He pulled his car in front of the woman's vehicle and started the short walk back toward her in the slow steady down pour. He felt the icy wetness almost instantly chill his flesh, beneath his crisp, white, uniform shirt, made him shiver. Even through the rainy darkness, he could see the glow of her blue green eyes, from her position behind the wheel. Without a word being said, he walked over to the driver's side of the compact car, wrenched the door handle and a flood poured out onto his feet. The moment was actually funny, until he realized that he was watching her dissolve right out the car door as well. A momentary laugh of hysterics escaped his lips, only seconds before the sputter of liquid shot first from his mouth then his nose. Then he himself began to dissolve into the rain, swirling down the street edge into a drain that read, "Hudson River Water Shed Access."

Countless revelers packed 7th Avenue & West 42nd Streets and beyond. There wasn't a parking space in sight. There was barely a place to stop for more than a second at a time. Anywhere, from the Hudson on the west side of Manhattan, to The FDR drive along the rivers east side was crowded. The mob was loud and rowdy, the excitement level was high and the citizens blended in, dressed like partiers, only with real guns instead of the infamous water pistols. City and public works officials decided to try something new this year, Instead of trying to seal off or swap out port-a-potties as they filled up.

They became unusable, as they quickly had in past gatherings; they connected them all via six inch flex tubes to a massive generator. This machine sucks the contents from the base of the port-a-potties through the tubes. Then down the street to a giant barge floating on the Hudson River just off of the Henry Hudson Parkway. This barge will serve as a floating holding tank for half of all of the port-a-potties in the Time Square vicinity. While a second barge, tied up along the sea wall on the east side of the Hudson River is used to store waste sucked from the remaining public toilets via a second generator and pumping station.

The technique worked like a charm the first time around. The only glitch in the process all night had been the port-a-potties manual locking system. The simple locks had to be turned manually from the interior. Once you entered, someone needs to secure the door and advise anyone waiting outside that this particular portable toilet was currently in use; but for some strange reason the doors kept ending up locked, with nobody inside. Figuring it a prank being pulled off by some drunken wise crack, young, unarmed, uniformed police guards had been assigned to monitor the ins and outs of the out houses. Security watched men and women go in and out at a steady pace.

Still one door or another was found to be mysteriously locked, each fifteen minutes or so throughout the night. It wasn't until a male recruit with OCD noticed that for every five males that had gone into the bathroom only three ladies went in. This might not have made much difference to anyone except to this cadet.

The amount of men exiting the port-a-potties is almost exact to the number of women coming out of the portable toilet. By the time the lighted crystal ball finally dropped on Time Square, The music had subsided. The local police officers started advising partiers that it was about that moment to clear the streets. The complex cadet was inexplicably sure that something fishy was going on in the big single unit. "Two hundred twelve men entered into these three urinals," but only two hundred two men came out," he said. "Two hundred and two women went in and all two hundred and two women exited" he stated dumbfounded. Nobody else paid that close attention to the comings and goings of people in the port-a-potties. No other person had noticed just how many men went into the ports tonight and not come out. After the celebrations concluded and the last of the rowdies hit the road, each of the potties were drained, disconnected and loaded onto flatbed trucks, empty. The Flex tubes were rolled onto the two separate barges, which would very early in the morning be tugged off to a New Jersey land field for permanent disposal.

WEDNESDAY, JANUARY 1ST 2013

By daybreak, the only thing rallying were the phone lines of the NYC 911 operators. A couple of calls came in for drunk and disorderlies and a few for vandalism, even some for stolen or damaged vehicles. By 10 AM they had received inquiries about two hundred and forty people unaccounted for. They're mostly friends, but a few from concerned relatives, pissed off girlfriends, mistresses or deceived wives. Of course they are told that they would have to wait 24 hours before they could file a missing persons report. There was very little the local authorities would be able to do at this time anyway. Seems they already had their hands full trying to avoid both a panic and a nightmare.

Under the circumstances, not one individual wanted to take the blame, for what might prove to be a big disaster. Nor did they want to believe there was any reason for coastal alarm along the east coast since Hurricane Sandy devastated the Jersey Shore. Both Barges, the first tied to a slip in front of the Jacob K Javits Convention Center, between the warehouses and the Holland Tunnel. The second barge had been docked on Manhattan's east side, just south of The United Nations Plaza Building and I-495. Both massive canal boats have now vanished.

Of course there were cameras all over New York City, Manhattan and the bridges that lead both in and out of the town. Not one showed movement on neither of the massive vessels parallel the riverside. Besides, with the number of Marine patrol units on the water, and several helicopter and a couple of blimps hovering over Time Square, how could you not have noticed two three hundred ton craft filled with sewage, drifting either north or south along the Hudson River? "Who would steal iron barges topped with rubbish?, was the question on everyone's mind, thought the police and Port Authority officials, to public works and of course the Environmental Protection Agency "Who would want to steal 20 tons of sewage and how could it be used to harm the citizens of this city?, the Mayor asked in an emergency lunch held in So Ho at noon. Marine Patrol units at the sights where the boats had been moored communicated back and forth across Manhattan by two-way radio; trying to figure out where forty plus tons of waste could have disappeared to.

"Well, look at the bright side," one waste management personnel was perceived to say "We won't have to pay to tow it to Jersey." "Maybe it just sank," said another public works employee. He all but chewed on the top of his thermos, seemingly trying desperately to cure his own hangover from the night before. The marine patrol officer heard this and suddenly got a terrific idea. Yanking the two-way radio off his belt he called to the other boat on the other end of the island, where the other barge had disappeared from. "M P 1 to MP 2 you copy"

"This is MP 2, Go ahead MP 1." "Hey Harry, you know we've tried everything from helicopters to high rise cameras looking for these two barges, I just had another idea, over." The two-way crackled and fell silent shortly before Harry replied. "At this point I feel like we've merely been pissing in the wind, so I'm about ready to try anything, what's on your mind Captain?" "Let's get some sonar in the water, what if those barges weren't stolen? What if they're down there?" he said. What if the damned things just sank?

Harry climbed into the 18 foot Dusky Marine patrol vessel, started the engine, untied the bowline, and pushed off from the dock. After maneuvering his boat until it was directly over the spot where the barge had been tied up, he cut the motor. That made it a little easier to hear what ever communications might come over his radio. Then he turned on the fish finder, which was all they had basically needed for searching the murky waters of the Hudson. Harry didn't notice anything at all resembling a trace of metal in the muddy waters of this river. What he saw fascinated him so much that he actually wet his pants.

The sonar showed, that Below Harry's boat and almost every liquid inch of water space around it, was now jammed with each kind and size of fish he'd ever known to be in this waterway. "Skates," was all Charlie said, over the radio, after walking to the starboard end of the craft and seeing for himself, the vast array of fish now spiraling around his boat. Even eels swirled in what he called a spaghetti ball of marine life, but no one caught him saying it. Harry had never seen anything like it in his over forty years of navigating in these waters; something he had learned to do off of the Long Island Sound with his father as a young boy. Refusing to believe his own eyes, he pulled up the right sleeve of his windbreaker.

He leaned over the side of the vessel, reached in and touched the swirling sphere of smooth, liquid. The fluid quickly spread up his arm and soaked his upper body before circulating into Harry's mouth, which hung open in amazement of the spectacle before him. In a matter of a few seconds, he was reduced to swirls of green water and becomes a part of the muddy Hudson. "M P 1 to MP 2 are you in position yet Harry?" The only thing he heard was the crackle of silence.

"M P 1 to MP 2, Harry you copy?" After trying several times to reach Harry by two way, he pulled his own boat over the area where the second barge had been tied up. He cut his engine so as to hear any communications that might come in over his radio. Then turned on the boat's fish finder and repeated Harry's actions, almost to the letter. Within a few minutes, a white F-150 pickup truck, baring the city's Department of public works logo with a strobe light, arrived on the site. It was south of The United Nations Building, where both a garbage barge and a Marine Patrol Officer in an 18 foot boat had been sitting only a short time ago. Finding no one at the given location, the two men came out of the truck and gathered at the sea wall and stared out over the top of the river. They were unaware that just below the surface, what had until only moments before been a worthy vessel, had now been stripped down to no more than microscopic particulates and a part of the massive water system.

One of the men suggested that maybe the man had to take a leak or something and that they should sit and wait for him to come back. At least long enough to enjoy a cigar. The other guy replied, "I kinda have to go myself, where are all those crappers when you need one?" After coming to a mutual consensus, the men decided to drive over to the other sight near the Jacob K Javits Convention Center, between the warehouses and the Holland Tunnel. They knew for sure they could find bathrooms and hot coffee on the other side.

When the two men riding in the pickup truck reached the east end of Manhattan, they basically found the same thing; an empty dock area, no boats, no cars, no trucks, no sign that anyone had been there recently.

Kick Off: 3:40 Central Time, 49ers @ Green bay playoff game -5 degrees, Wind Chills up to - 20 degrees. The arena gave free hot beverages to the hordes of people pouring into the stadium from cars, trucks, Busses and SUVs that poured in from Military Avenue onto Lombardi Street, in anticipation of the big sport. Diehard fans had packed not only the expensive field's parking spaces, but also each space in every local park within a five-mile radius as well. The normal pre-game tailgate parties weren't even thought about, as temperatures hovered below freezing. A regional store gave away 70,000 hand warmers at no cost. It literally still had been either team's match right down to the final seconds. As soon as the last score went up, both the men and ladies' rooms began to pump out water at a combined capacity of over 400 gallons per minute. Urinals and toilets flushed the alcohol consumed over the past four hours that they spent at Lambeau field.

As the trickle began to lighten and fans departed for the packed parking lots, nobody noticed a young man carrying a third of a cup of beer in one hand and about two pounds of nachos and chili peppers in the other. It caused his stomach to boil, as he rushed frantically into the furthest stall.

While trying desperately to drop his pants without dropping his ale, the guy was in a hurry to get to the toilet, that he hadn't even bothered securing the manual latch on the door. It wouldn't have mattered, if he locked it, since he was the only one currently in the bathroom anyway. As he noisily emptied his bowels in the end stall, he gave a sigh of relief, as a long held stream of urine rained into the porcelain bowl. But all was not normal on this day. While he was sitting there, the man felt a cold splash against his hairy bottom and jumped up almost as quickly as he'd sat down.

But it was already too late for the next unknowing victim. Before he could even let out so much as a scream; his body was liquefied and seemingly flushed down the mouth of the handicap toilet. A few minutes later another man, looking to be about the same age as the one before, walked noisily into the men's room; "Hey Aaron, what the hell man, you flush your balls by accident, or what?" After hearing only the sound of the stadium's ceiling speaker, the guy called out yet again; "Aaron, you in here?" he asked, as he made his way toward a urinal to relieve his own urges.

The young male undid his zipper, allowing his manhood to fall forward into it. He hated the idea of his own pee splashing back on him as he voided. He reached up and activated the automatic flush, which caused a noise like nothing he'd ever heard, or would hear again. Instead of backsplash, what he got was a full-fledged soaking from head to toe by the thick acrid, green sewer water. The young man threw up both hands and opened his mouth in protest, allowing the smelly liquid the approach it apparently needed. The Next two patrons walked in as the sound of the flushing urinal had relinquished, they found nothing out of the ordinary. The first patron went straight to the bowl with the acrid green water, the second strolled to the last stall, the one marked "Handicapped Access"

THE POLAR VORTEX - WINTER STORM ION

Winter came in with a vengeance, and blizzard warnings covered most of the northern U.S., from as far west as Minneapolis-St. Paul Minnesota, where temperatures hovered right around -20 for almost a week. To the mid-west, Firemen in Devil's Lake North Dakota tried fighting flames with snow when the Dakota Dried Bean Storage at the lake caught fire. Two firefighters suffered frost bite trying to extinguish the blaze. Lake front cities like Chicago were glad that they had decided to cancel school in preparation for winter storm Ion. More than 500 passengers on 3 locomotives spent 9 hours stuck on trains in Northern Illinois after sleet concealed and then blocked tracks outside of the windy city. Commuters were warm and had plenty of supplies and were eventually bussed into Chi-town. Triple A in Chicago was flooded with over 600 calls per hour, from motorist whose cars refused to start in this deep freeze. With recorded temperatures like thirty below zero in places such as Rice Lake Wisconsin, with wind-chills of minus fifty-five and daily high temps around twelve degrees, people hunkered down and waited out what was now being called Winter Storm Ion. Lake Superior, Michigan, Huron, Erie and Ontario, had all already frozen, with more than two months of winter still remaining, as water freezes it will also expand, as the great lakes froze.

So did the breakers that usually beat long the hundreds of miles of sea wall. The storms strong winds soon pushed the massive buildup of snow east. Enormous ice jams piled up along the eastern shores, threatening to over flow the shorelines and overtake towns in Sackets Harbor.

West of Watertown off of Lake Ontario and Oswego New York, the Oswego river inlet first iced, then rose as it traveled south into Onondaga Lake in Liverpool, north of Syracuse. The resulting ice jam there muddled along to push the frozen sheets so far out of the cove that it had managed to all but devour the surrounding area. It, completely decimating expensive homes along the eastern shore of the bay, on Onondaga Lake trail. Police, fire and other available emergency personnel were ordered to evacuate everyone between Onondaga sound and the I-90 New York State Thruway on the east side. Every person along the two miles of I-690 on the west side of the lake and I-690 and I-81 south were also evacuated.

The almost exact same scenario was taking place in Buffalo New York, where the Niagara River fed Lake Erie into Lake Ontario, by way of Niagara Falls. The St. Lawrence basin usually carries water from Lake Erie, North east between Wolfe Island Canada and Chaumont Bay in the

U.S., where Lake Erie feeds into St. Lawrence. It then flows north east along Montreal before opening into The Gulf of St. Lawrence, where it would flow past New Brunswick and Prince Edward Isle. It then connects with the cold Atlantic Ocean in the Cabot Straits. From the Atlantic it depends on the jet stream and trade winds, whether the waters continue north to the Labrador Sea, where it would eventually feed into the Arctic Ocean, or continued east to the European, Africa and Asian coast. Nobody realized that on January 7, exactly seven days into the New Year, conditions would cause all the waters of the earth to rise and connect, becoming one body of water, for the first time since the continents had divided, thousands of years ago. The remaining particulates from the two barges that had vanished from The Hudson on both sides of Manhattan had now made their path as far west as The Bearing Straights which separated Russia from Alaska and The North Pole from The Pacific.

JANUARY - WEEK TWO

The grandson of the founder of Vale Colorado became the fifth person in the rocky mountain region to reportedly die in an avalanche this winter's ski season. What wasn't reported to the media was, a snow show wearing naturalist that had been hiking along the Rockies on an exploration to find inner peace. He stumbled upon a waterfall that seemed to go against everything he had seen since he arrived at the Holy Cross City on his journey Mount of the Holy Cross. He filled his water bottle in Honky Dory reservoir, which was the first lake he had come across after arriving at the mountain's base. The historian found the trip up the snowy landscape arduous at times, but with his eyes on their prize, the summit of Mount of the Holy Cross. Most of his trek toward the peak had been made in snow shoes. He was thankful to have exchanged them for a set of Sony Hi-Fi radio headphones that he never got to use anyway.

The tattered map, that he kept in the inside pocket of the old army jacket, he basically lived in for the past few months, assured him that the next watering hole, Seven Sisters lake, was only about a mile further not far from where he was standing. He could now hear the sound of running water ahead, which caused him to quicken his step. He sang a little tune as he came around a cliff face into a clearing that he might have described as, beautiful beyond words.

The water flowing down from the rocks had turned almost fully into steam as soon as it moved close into contact with the nearly frozen soil in the stream below.

The weary traveler steadied his heavy back pack and bed roll atop a large boulder, being careful to place it where it would remain dry. A quick dip of his fingers into the sparkling clear water let him know that the water was a comfortable eighty-two degrees. Perfect bathing temperature and being that he hadn't had a shower in over a month, he wasted little time walking directly in, totally clothed. "Hot Dam, clean my clothes and a cleansing, no charge" the guy stated as he fully lowered himself in the steam stream. The nearly scorching water was exactly what he needed to both reinvigorate his physique and cleanse both it and his clothing. Leaning back in the sultry water, now almost entirely underneath, he said quietly to himself, "I could die right here." After a few minutes of total body warmth and relaxation, the historian noticed himself dozing off. He thought to himself, "I'd best get myself moving, or that last statement just might come true sooner than later. It was then that he sensed what felt to him like a warm ocean breeze. The mild gust seemed to be approaching from behind the waterfall. Rather than rising up out of the tepid water to go survey where the summary air was advancing from, he quickly decided to remain submerged, doggy paddling his way over to the very edge of the falls. The Man dived in completely, coming up on the other side of the cascade. What he saw there made him instantly giddy.

The underground chamber was lined with large purple jewels, which seemed to shine a path, deep into the caves underbelly. "Holy hot rocks bat man" the guy said to himself. He worked his way even deeper into the grotto, now in total awe of what he had already come to call his, find of a lifetime. He reached up and ran his fingertips over one of the larger glowing stones. The naturalist noticed what he thought was a shadow, caused by his fingers momentarily cancelling out the stone's eerie iridescent light. Realizing how loosely the stone sat in the rock, the male extended his hand up again. He extracted the gem this time from its place on the cave wall and jammed it into the tattered pockets of his drab olive army jacket. He then reached up with both hands and began picking stones at an astronomical rate.

Not realizing that each gem he pulled and plucked had caused the entrance of the cavern to grow darker and darker. Before long, he had made his way deep into the mouth of the cave and behind him, total darkness. He presently found that he was in total murkiness and realized that he was not alone.

JANUARY 9, 6:20PM.

The solar storm that's been hurtling a billion tons of material toward our planet, at two million miles per hour, is now slamming into Earth's atmosphere, NOAA's Space Weather Prediction Center tells ABC News. For the next 24 hours forecasters say a "strong" geomagnetic storm could cause navigation and frequency problems for satellites, communication dropouts for ships and planes in Polar Regions, and might affect GPS systems and satellite radio. Airlines are already avoiding polar routes to keep passengers and crew from elevated levels of radiation.

"It's significant, but it's not the mother of all storms," said NOAA space scientist Joe Kunches. "The good news is that people with GPS in their cars probably won't see much of an effect." Kunches says. The aurora will also be seen further south than normal. These Solar winds are rated like hurricanes, and the geomagnetic storm hitting now is considered an "S-3," in the middle of the scale, with 5 being the most extreme. Our planet isn't out of the woods yet. The area of the Sun where this storm originated 48 hours ago will still be a threat for about another week until it rotates away from Earth," he stated. "Polar

Regions are especially affected. If this whirlwind had occurred during last week's rescue attempt of researchers stuck in ice near Antarctica, communications would have likely been severely impacted," he announced. NASA postponed a launch from Virginia's eastern shore of the Cygnus cargo spacecraft, scheduled to deliver supplies to the International Space Station, because of the radiation. Cygnus launched today and is planned to arrive at the terminal early Sunday. Very little affect was discerned in modern society's electronic landscape over the storms 24 hour rein. People sat huddled around their fireplace and flat screen TV's, manufacturing fat as they had done for years. But out in the ocean, the radiation from the massive geomagnetic storm was causing the oceans to glow a bright iridescence, usually only seen under black light. Miles below the surface of the sea, what could only be described as undersea lightning bolts, triangulated vectors that is set in a direct conflict with the destruction of all mankind. In fact, all fouls and mammalian life as we know it would cease to exist. Although the waters of all four of the Great Lakes were currently frozen, both the seed and the scene is now in motion.

To the many spectators that dared to brave the cold to see the famed Niagara Falls, this first week of the year an arctic gale had even silenced the chute. It left thousands upon thousands of giant icicles hanging over its now silent crest. Just below, an unseen and unforeseen change is taking place. Microscopic organisms are connecting like freaks at an orgy, multiplying at an unimaginable rate. Had anyone been flying high above the frozen precipitation and took notice, they might have in fact seen the hue beneath the ice. It actually changed from a deep green to an unbelievable blue. Since seventy percent of the earth's surface is water, the change would be felt worldwide and fearfully soon.

JANUARY 10TH DAY BREAK

Residences all over West Virginia scrambled to buy bottled water as a major chemical leak, from a large industrial tank, had somehow ruptured. It is leaking an unknown amount of 4-Methylcyclohexane Methanol, or Crude MCHM. A chemical used in the coal industry, running into the main water supply. All the residents had been advised not to use the water in any capacity, even after boiling. First thing that morning, immediately after the news, there had been a run on bottled water, all over the state.

FRIDAY, JANUARY 10, 3:06 P.M. CST, THE ELK RIVER

CHARLESTON, W., Virginia (Reuters) - Up to 300,000 West Virginia residents were told not to drink tap water on Friday after a chemical spill called its safety into question. Health officials said water in the affected area should only be used for flushing toilets and fighting fires. "We don't know that the water's not safe, but I can't say it's not harmful," Jeff McIntyre, president of West Virginia American Water Co, told a televised news conference. The company runs the state's largest water treatment plant. Water is distributed to residents at the South Charleston Community Center in Charleston. W.V. Governor Earl Ray Tomblin declared a state of emergency for nine counties, and President Barack Obama issued an urgent declaration on Friday. The spillage forced the closure of schools and businesses in the state capital. Tests were being done on the water, McIntyre said, but he could not say when it would be proclaimed safe for normal use.

The spillover of 4-Methylcyclohexane Methanol, an element used in the coal industry, occurred on Thursday on the Elk River in Charleston, Virginia's paramount. It is the largest city, upriver from the plant run by West Virginia American Water. Water carrying this component has an odor like licorice or anise, McIntyre said. The constituent is not highly lethal. Since the firm does not regularly see it as a contaminant, the level that could be considered safe has yet to be quantified, he said.

An agency spokeswoman said the ingredient potentially may be harmful if swallowed and may cause skin and eye irritation.

The chemical spill originated at Freedom Industries, a Charleston organization that produces specialty chemicals for the mining, steel and cements industries.

Freedom Industries President Gary Southern said in a statement, that the company was still determining how much Crude MCHM had been released. "Our team has been working around the clock since the discovery, to contain the leak and prevent further contamination," he said. Emergency workers and American Water distributed fresh water to centers surrounding the affected area. Residents formed extended lines at stores and quickly depleted inventories of bottled water. "It's just ridiculous. There's nowhere to buy water and everywhere seems to be sold out. This isn't going to endure two days," said the resident of Charleston, who was buying the last of the jugs of water at a Wal-Mart store. Another Charleston occupant even considered heading out of town for the weekend. "I'm not sure how long I can go without a shower. This is unbearable," she said. The Kanawha-Charleston and the Putnam County Health Departments ordered the closure of all restaurants and schools receiving water from the West Virginia American Water company. Colleges were also closed in many counties, including Boone, Cabell, Clay, Jackson, Kanawha, Lincoln, Pocahontas and Putnam.

The spill was discovered after the West Virginia Department of Environmental Protection received a report of a strange odor on Thursday morning. They visited the Freedom Industries site, where they found a leaking storage unit, a spokeswoman for Governor Tomblin said.

(Additional reporting by Ian Simpson in Washington, Mary Wisniewski in Chicago and Eric M. Johnson in Seattle; Editing by Eric Walsh, Stephen Powell, Toni Reinhold) Copyright © 2014, Reuters The 4-Methylcyclohexane Methanol, had not been let out in a massive number, but what was released, had been timed perfectly to alter both the chemical and genetic makeup of organisms now multiplying in mind shattering numbers just beneath the surface of the frozen waters.

Once again, microscopic particles mate and transform. Creating and forming a substance that could divide to become multiple substances. Each was capable of thought, or combined to turn into a single element. It also has the ability of unforeseen savagery against not only mankind, but the globe as a whole. After it had required the 4-Methylcyclohexane Methanol, needed from the West Virginia spill, the solar geomagnetic storm provided it the radiation essential to energize the nucleus of a predominantly unstoppable species.

That evening looked normal on thirty percent of earth, populated by both mankind and mammal alike. By the morning it would become quite clear that during the night, something had gone terribly wrong. A sailor aboard The U.S. Navy destroyer Lawrence, was returning to the states after an eight month Mediterranean cruise. While doing his roving patrol duties, he reported seeing a human body in the water off of the ships starboard bow.

He instantly announced the sighting to the helmsman and other officers in the wheel house and the sailor at the helm was ordered now to turn about, all engines slow. As the ship returned to look for what looked to be a plump graying corps in a cluster of green seaweed. A six man crew donned life jackets before climbing into a compact life boat, being lowered into the ocean and making their way out to the bloated clump in the tangle of sea grass. The sailors paddled the boat out to and up along the mass. After donning heavy latex gloves, one of the seamen reached out with a gaffing peg to pull the frame alongside and secure it to the small vessel. No sooner than the seaman holding the hook touched the gray puffy grey heap all hell broke loose. From what can be seen waiting near the rails, something appearing to have bulging dark eyes and thin like fingers flipped the little craft and took the six men and the boat below the surface.

The crew of the Navy vessel sprang into action at once; some even dove instantly into the freezing Atlantic waters to try to somehow aid their fellow sailors. Another boat was deployed at once to help everyone that was presently in the cold sea of the Mediterranean. The men swam anxiously toward where the six men had gone under only seconds earlier. Some of the men were right away diving, in search of their missing shipmates.

After several dives and what almost amounted to mass panic, the form returned to the surface, about forty nautical yards from where it had went down. A second life boat team was alerted and immediately deployed and made its way toward the now totally still and faced down figure, drifting off of the starboard bow. As the men paddled feverishly to get to the lone body, so to render whatever aid might be needed, other bodies began to pop up all about them.

All six men were now surfacing face down all around the boatmen in the small row boat. Sailors that had actually jumped overboard into the sea, from the ship had already begun to arrive at the location of their floating comrades. They were trying desperately to keep each man's head out of the water.

The main person to be pulled from the deep was a boats mate first class, who was both pale gray, ice cold. His skin felt paper thin as they drew him up on the first lifeboat; his ashy complexion looked as though it might already be too late for CPR. It took several of them to pull this now limp body over the side and into the small inflatable. This exact scene played out over and over with each, until the only remaining man had finally been pulled from the sea. The six lifeless figures were all hoisted onto the deck of the ship where medical corpsmen rendered immediate attention to each.

It is quickly determined that each of the men were beyond help and declared to have died by drowning. The males are taken below deck to the ships clinic where their bodies are prepared for return to the U.S. for burial. Their bunkmates are assigned to clear out their lockers and strip their racks before they arrived in home port. They have not been on leave since August of last year. The seamen had all been in a jubilant mood, right up until the unfortunate incident.

As the ship set a course, full steam ahead, toward the U.S. Southern coastline, division officers for the fallen, attempted to prepare documentation explaining how and why six of their sailors were now below deck in cold storage. As the Navy destroyer was lead into port by tug boats, the crew prepared to debark on American soil for the first time in half a year.

All of a sudden chaos broke out on the bottom level of the boat. It caused sirens to sound and the intercom to announce, "Now hear this, Master at Arms please report to the Medic A.s.a.p. This is not a drill I repeat, this is not a drill." The calm had once again turned frantic. Personnel scrambled to their duty stations and to lower decks in response to the orders being blared over the ship's blaring PA system. Below deck ship security officers and medics gathered throughout the doors of the ships examiner's office. Soon after declaring the six fellow craft mates deceased, the Chief health official asked the corpsmen to wrap each of them in clean white sheets and store them in the cold storage locker. After thinking he'd heard a noise coming from the icy reserved locked unit, the medical officer looked in through a small window. At the top of the door he was dumbfounded to see five of the half a dozen male huddled on the floor in the corner of the room. Their linen was wrapped around their naked bodies like warm blankets. The sixth man was still lying on a gurney in the far section, but he too had apparently woken up at some point.

For at the moment he lay curled in a fetal position, suckling the thumb stuck deeply in his mouth. "What the hell is going on?" The Chief Master at Arms bellowed. Then, he noticed the men that were all thought to be dead, only a short time ago, now alive and well again. But something wasn't quite right. The MAA observed first that the sailor on the litter was not sucking his finger after all, he was evidently eating it, but there was no blood from the wound.

Shortly after, the ships lines were secured at Pier 18, where several ambulances, paramedics and Navy shore patrol stood waiting. Bells rang out on the dock as the massive, tracked crane maneuvered the heavy, metal gangplank into position. As soon as the stave was fastened and the crane's cables had been removed, six stretchers were guided by two medical personnel. Piled high with electronic emergency equipment, medics scurried up the gang plank and through the first gray triple-z dogged door on the ship's bulkhead. EMS had to leave their gurneys in the hallway. They followed the crew members down a ladder to the Dispensary where the men had each been wrapped and stored in the boats morgue.

"Attention on deck" one of the lower class officers yelled, as the higher ranking officer with the twin gold bars on his collar entered the small space via the stepladder. "As you were," he snapped back as the others followed him carefully down the steps into the little room. As the official made his way toward the crew members, he couldn't help but see, what he thought to be sorrow in their faces. They were all crying for the fallen shipmates, until the MAA spoke up.

'Sir, you're never going to believe this," he said. He was even more excited than he'd been when he'd single handedly captured a well-armed Somali pirate. A marauder, who somehow managed to make his way onto an underway U.S. Navy Destroyer. Without opening it, the MAA stepped backward from the door, allowing the boatman to look in, still not attempting to unlock the doors. The Official glanced quickly into the small window before yelling, "Is this somebody's idea of a goddamned joke? Open it!" he said. Stepping back momentarily, the MAA stuck the large brass key into the lock and turned it sharply until it clicked loudly and then yanked on the door. He followed on the heels of the officer as he entered the cold storage. There were five of his crewmen, at the moment, huddled together naked on the floor in the corner. A sixth crew member still lay curled in a fetal position atop a gurney near a rear bulk head. The military personnel and the MAA literally stepped over the other men and headed straight away for the sailor on the litter. Only then, did the young seaman notice that the male had eaten off all but two of his fingers. He was again gnawing at what was left of his hand.

The lack of blood around the area of the now missing digits was not as much of a concern as the health and wellbeing of every single man on this vessel. Instinct and adrenalin both kicked in at once and the official grabbed for the man's wrist, in an attempt to keep him from doing any further damage. What happened next was not expected, seen or recorded by anyone as there were no surviving witnesses. What the mariner grasped did not feel like human skin at all. It seemed similar to that of the marlin he caught once on shore leave, off of the Caiman Islands. Before he could utter a solitary word of disbelief, he watched this thing on the ship; turn into what now looked comparable to a mass of swirling bubbles right before his eyes. A heap was then beginning to swirl upward surrounding his arm. The sailor parted his lips to say something.

Then the foam quickly filled first his mouth and the mouth of the MAA which had been hanging wide open in total astonishment. In fact, before anyone in the lower compartment, medics included, could take any kind of defensive action, the whole room became flooded with a thick, whirl of blue-green slime. The ooze immediately devoured everyone and the contents in the area, including all six men. The substance swirled faster and faster, seemingly emulsifying everything, until all that was left was cold, swirling water. The liquid then poured upward over the ladder and through the opening. On the main deck of the ship, it then ran over the side like water from a busted rain gutter back into the sea from whence it had originally come. Within a matter of seconds, the door on a Port-A-Potty, less than a hundred yards from the boat opened. Out walked a young officer sporting a camouflage navy uniform. The insignia on the collar showed two gold bars. The man had made it only a few feet from the outhouse and seemed to be adjusting his outfit when the entry to the potty swung open once again. This time, producing a slim guy in a blue khaki work jumper, who strolled out and quickly joined up with the boatman now waiting outside. The entrance to the Portable toilet unbolted yet again; and the scenario repeated itself, until each of the men that had been inside the cramped space, now all stood together again once again, on Pier 18. The seaman, the MAA and his assistant, escorted the twelve paramedics once again up the ship's gangplank, without ever raising the suspicions of the watch officers or any of the ships crewmen. The sailor, wearing a large duty belt and a holstered side arm, popped to attention as the officer ascended on board and honored him with a full hand salute. The officer in return saluted both he and the Union Jack. The banner was gently swaying in the breeze from the flag pole aft as he and the paramedics once again boarded the craft.

The twelve medics quickly retrieved the six gurneys left on the ship's main deck, before descending back down the gang plank to their six waiting, empty ambulances. Not until the ambulances had cleared the pier, did the ship's intercom sound. It started with the toning of the bell. Then, an excited voice announcing, "Liberty call, liberty call, all extra personnel not muster on the fantail with the duty Master at Arms; the smoking lamp is now lit in all compartments where smoking is permitted." This message was followed by the hoots and hoopla's of many men who had not seen friends, family members, loved ones, or beloved country since they'd departed on Independence Day. The six

Ambulances formed what would have looked to anyone who might have noticed, like an emergency caravan. A convoy it was, but a fleet for something even more sinister. As the underlings now had the stockpile of medicines they would need to heal the half human infants that the women were delivering in mind boggling numbers. For the first few hours after birth, the semi humanoid babies needed much more maintenance than newborns of their own kind, basically after some time of being born. The human infant also showed signs of having problems adjusting to altitude and depth difference, as well as temperature change and aqua infusion. Since regular underling children could be found many nautical miles from their birthing places within hours of their birth, the "Halfies" as they would for a short time come to be known, seemed satisfied with staying put in the place where they were conceived.

The Halfies as well appeared to have a higher food intake.

They seemingly stored a lofty fat content, causing the few that had gained full aqua infusion to have a problem with buoyance. The last trial to integrate the topmost species with the subspecies nonetheless, had gone far better than it had the times before. Mankind as it were on the outside continued as usual. Children walk into schools and shoot fellow classmates, rape and rob them, show hatred and jealousy and have nothing but pure prejudice for its own kind. Not to mention this breed was the only one on the planet that needed to destroy its habitat and rebuild it to make itself comfortable. Elk, grizzly bear, and every whale of its kind were suitable to its territory. Even the massive silver backed gorilla of the rainforest, the creature most like the surface dweller had adapted to its surroundings. The top dwellers however felt that everything in their environment was put there to somehow give service to and comfort them.

Now the underlings (also born here) were now just about ready to fight back. They forged to save what they presently called their home as well; after all, it was the place of their birth.

Thanks to Internet Networks namely Facebook, Google, Twitter and the like, the world was now abuzz about the newest on line sensation. Around the globe, rumors had it that someone took a picture with their cell phone, and shared it on the web. It was an image that within forty eight hours had gone viral. "The best damned hoax I've ever seen," stated Jason Mercado, film critique and longtime editor journalist. "I mean if this is real, do you have any idea what this means?" he continued in an almost euphoric though giddy undertone. "As I said, all of the trillions of not only dollars, but the amount of time we've spent looking for alternate life in space. All the while, all these years, they've been in our oceans. Unencumbered and reproducing, just beyond our vision, our realm, our scope of knowledge and our ability to believe."

The U.S. Secret Service tried immediately, although behind schedule, to confiscate the video. Thereby heading off an uprising and realizing at once that it was long past too late to hide the visual images. Within hours, they had comprised a story so good that had other government agencies eating it up.

They claimed that the Navy had been testing a special dive suit, one that would make them not only less detectable to the enemy, but was lighter and fully self-contained. This new suit was said to be so advanced that the diver actually was able to reuse his own oxygen. The odorless gas was recirculated back into filters built into the ensemble itself, making the diver's job less cumbersome and allowed their swimming ability seem more natural. But the residents weren't taking the bait this time around. People turned out on the waters in anything that they could get to float. Everything from monster mega-yachts to one person kayaks. An older guy even showed up on the beach front in a decrepit Ford Falcon pulling a camper that had to be as ancient as the junker itself. The matching chrome bubble rims on both the hoary falcon and the trailer rusted probably many years ago. In the rear of the home-made pup tent sat a homemade, makeshift raft. He constructed the float of corrugated metal roofing and what looked like over a hundred plastic milk jugs, tied together with duct tape. Both cops and state park officials argued with the elder that the craft was not safe for him or other vessels on the harbor. The fellow refused to listen and continued to attempt to put the contraption into the water. Until police cited him for having expired tags on the station wagon and no tags at all on the caravan. The tags on the vehicle had in fact been invalid since 1973. Further investigation established that the man's license, which they found in the almost corroded shut glove box of the old jalopy, had also lapsed in that same year.

At this time the deputy, who hadn't even been born until 1979 decided to detain the elder until he could get a better idea of who he was, and determine if he had actually acquired a driver's license in the past forty years. It was at that moment that the young cop got a call on his radio of a collision between a jet ski and a fishing boat near his position. Thinking that his chances of impressing some bikini clad hottie was probably going to be better on the other call, the officer informed the man once again firmly, "I want you to hold up right here until another agent gets here to check out your credentials" he told the old male. "To make sure you wait for him, I'm keeping this," the official stated as he let the aged fella see that he was pocketing his forty year expired document. Then just to be certain, the officer cuffed one of the man's wrists to the steel bar of his decrepit trailer. That being done, the fed ordered the senior to stay there and he and the state park ranger jaunted off toward the shoreline to the jetties. As soon as they had made their way down the shore, the geezer raised his arm with the cuff. The shackles passed through his wrist and the metal railing of his camper and dropped with an unheard clink to the sandy beach below. The old man then walked quietly over to his vehicle and cranked it up. He put it in reverse and backed both the car and trailer into the river. Then he, the falcon, its camper and the homemade boat had all disappeared below the surface of the water.

FRIDAY DECEMBER 17TH, 5:48 PM.
THE RUSTY ANCHOR SALOON

Richard sat alone in the large parking lot outside the Rusty Anchor. He thought back over what seemed to him, to have been a tremendously long work week, even though he had an extra shift off during the week, because he worked this Saturday. In reality he felt like he was still sitting there more out of habit than anything else. Back in the day it would have been right about now that Carl would tap the corner of his military 1st gunnery. With his pinky ring he would tap against the rear window and say something stupid like, "This is the police, keep your hands where I can see them." Rich missed Carl; in fact he is missing each and every one of the guys from the old crew. Meanwhile, until this day, nobody seems to have a clue what happened to the six of them. Neither of them even seemed to have relatives that could be contacted to come get their personal belongings from their lockers back at the shop.

Figuring he was sure to get more details when he kept the court date now looming ahead of him like a dark nemeses from a different dimension. Richard wasn't much of a drinker. In fact two would usually do, but after one he was probably done. He knew that his job depended on his ability to operate a motor vehicle; therefore he would never do anything to jeopardize that, contrary to popular beliefs at the moment.

Rich removed his debit card from his billfold, placing the plastic in his right front pant pocket and his wallet in the glove compartment of his motorcar. After checking all of the doors and windows, again more or less out of habit, since his car had power windows and door locks, Rich stepped out of the auto, making his path across the large parking lot alone. He immediately asked himself why he had parked all the way over by the seawall, instead of closer to the building. He had actually answered himself out loud, muttering under his breath, "a force of habit." As he walked the thirty yards or so to the establishment, Rich couldn't help but see out of the corner of his eye, six women, also walking toward the entrance of the business. Without even noticing it, he licked his fingers before running them through his hair, using the nearest parked vehicle to check his reflection in the car's side window.

Rich also would have sworn that he didn't take any added pep in his step either. Somehow he managed to overtake the women, before they reached the entrance to the establishment. Like a true gentleman, he actually nodded as he held the door for each of them. His head bowed in a gesture that said, I'm not worthy to make eye contact with beauty so fair. He kept his head down until the final one, and the shortest of the six of them crossed over the threshold.

The bar was instantly filled with the hoopla and cat calls from the hard working and even harder regulars that called The Anchor home on Friday nights. Richard remained with his gaze lowered and deprived himself of the view that was apparently driving the men in the barroom bonkers at this very moment. He noticed something else that he himself thought strange. Richard figured it had to have been either the lighting of the setting sun playing tricks on his eyes, as it cut through the beveled angles of the wood and glass entry doors. It caused a prism of light to scatter across both the floor and the women's seemingly extra tiny feet. Rich stepped in last, behind the six and had to press his palm into the back of the last lady to enter. They all stopped just inside of the building and they went no further.

Rich pressed his palm gently into the small of her spine. He let her know that he had wanted to squeeze past. Then the feeling of her curved spinal column totally escaped his touch. This too was quickly forgotten, as she turned and looked at him with the most golden skin and bluest eyes Rich had ever seen and a deep cleft in her top lip. Richard stood motionless as the six now seemingly floated on by.

PART II "THE SPAWNING" - SATURDAY, JANUARY 18

Fishermen everywhere were reporting record catches. From the massive trawlers hauling their heavy nets and baskets of Opilio, Snow, King and Dungeness crabs, all the way down to the brook, or streams and watering holes, yards and remote, out of the way places. Young and old alike were enjoying casting again as fishing licenses sold widespread in record numbers. Ethel Benefield, a long time fisherwoman from Wrens Georgia was known as Aunt May to Wrens Georgia locals. She told Augusta news station WFXG, "It's almost like the fish are tired of being in the creek. Now they're all anxious to get out." The same scenario is now playing out from the oceans to the everglades. The same was happening in reservoirs, rivers and creeks all over the world. From catfish in The Congo to Piranha in the Paraguay basin of the coastal inlets of northeastern Brazil, The run on fish, crab and other sea favorites made headlines worldwide.

Boat captains around the globe, were all recording big catches, and water's edge trawlers were pulling them in as fast as they could cast their lines into the briny. Even in the freezing waters of the Great Lakes, anglers were finding that all you had to do was drill a few trenches in the frozen water. Then all you had to do was step back, wait and watch. Within a matter of seconds of the hole being cut and opened, fish began jumping out of the ditch onto the hard packed ice. This amazing scene was captured on cell phones and shared on You-Tube and Facebook in astronomical numbers. This new run on easy catch did however cause another problem, a sharp drop in seafood prices. Seafood had now become so plentiful that the price of lobster had now dropped to a dollar a pound. Jumbo shrimp were literally selling for as little as ten cents each. Road side venders that usually sold beef tacos and burritos are now selling lobster burritos and lump crab meat and tilapia taco. Few asked why the seas were now giving up their bounty. Many took from her the harvest of the sea, not once considering the reasoning behind or the repercussions of the ocean's own actions. Of course the NOAA (National Oceanic and Atmospheric Administration) and the Navy had to know what the real cause of this super bowl of seafood was and they too soon had their boats in the water with all of their expensive asdic and other deep sea seeking instruments. The second the underwater cameras were turned on, the sonar technician's jaws dropped in utter amazement. It was nothing any of them had ever seen before. A sonar tech who retired from the navy, before he began working with the NOAA said that he has never seen anything like this in his entire life in the ocean. He grew up in Penobscot Bay and he and his family etched out their living from the briny, diving, fishing, and caging massive Main lobster.

What he saw beneath the boat when the video came on literally scared the bejesus out of him. Everything from giant isopods to sand shrimp, seahorses, shark, salmon, swordfish, turtles, tarpon, grouper, jewfish and jellyfish, now swarmed in a gooey, almost soup like sauce, just below the surface of the waters. It was at this point that the captain of the NOAA vessel put the bathysphere into the water. The bathometer was a tiny, two-man, self-contained submarine that could have them right in the thick of it within a matter of minutes. Seeing this as somewhat of a historic event, the skipper decided to actually be one of the men to go into in the submersible. But what they observed was not recorded and they were never seen again.

"THE THAW"

Within half an hour the Coast Guard had totally cordoned off the area by boat access and Marine patrol and local police were denying anyone entry by land. Within a couple of hours the Navy had blocked off an even larger section of ocean, this one covering over five hundred nautical miles. The Navy released its first depth charge promptly at 4PM. An officer aboard the Destroyer (DDG) dropped the charge and was quoted saying, "we've tried playing nice now let's show them what happens when you mess with the best." The repercussions of the depth charge's concussion had an almost instantaneous affect. As the first ripples reached the beach, so did the first small remnants of sea life. An almost microscopic organism, that was once dead, looked like nothing more than pink gray foam on the water's veneer. Seemingly, the initial blast had done little more than disturb the kelp and other smaller microorganisms that had long fed the marine life along the beaches, aquatic life that now lay either stunned, lost or dying just below the surface.

By daybreak, visible signs of the depth charges destruction could be seen along the beach fronts for miles. Everything from octopi, eels and a mind boggling array of sea life and fish of every imaginable color had washed up along the beaches for as far as the human eye could see. Scorns of seabirds had begun scavenging the carcasses Strewn along the shores by daylight, the two men lay dead among the carnage by the time the sun had cleared the surface of the eastern beaches. The scene on the ground was startling, but the sight from the crew of the news helicopter flying overhead was too gut wrenching to say the least. Miles and miles of coastline was now covered with dead purpose's, rays, sharks, turtles and even a few deep water game fish like dolphin, grouper and marlin. The brash, young reporter ordered the captain of the chopper to move in the vicinity and hover, so that the photographer could give their news audience an up close and personal opinion of what was sure to make him an award winning journalist.

But the odor was too overwhelming and he soon all but begged the pilot to pull up for a wide angled view. The smell of death had gotten so strong in the copter the commander said, that he could actually feel it against his skin. As he raised the chopper, giving himself and the crew a breath of fresh air and an almost panoramic view, being a seasoned flyer, he thought he'd noted a subtle change or difference in the hue of the sea as they hovered above it just after sunrise. The briny had gone from its normal blissful blue, to a cold gray-green. As the captain allowed the helicopter to rise still higher over the ocean currents, he couldn't help but look up in the direction of the massive cloud that he knew without a doubt would be there above the copter, but there wasn't overcast in the morning sky. Now allowing his eyes to slowly follow the silhouette of what he had thought until only a few seconds ago, was a cloud formation above them, the pilot noticed it wasn't floating in the atmosphere above the water surface at all; it was precisely beneath the surface of the water. He couldn't judge the size of it for sure, but he realized for certain that whatever it was, it was too big to be a fish. "You see that?" the commander yelled back toward the journalist who was trying to direct the photographer as to what angle would best display the all-around immenseness of the situation, while still capturing his good side. "See what?" the reporter screamed back as he looked out in the direction in which the pilots head was turned. It was at that moment that all three of them saw what appeared to be like a heavy rain shower, coming directly towards them, only it seemed to be advancing up out of the ocean. The cameraman instinctively aimed and focused his camera for what's known in the business as the money shot as the hydrous hand pulled them from the sky.

Being in a hurry to get to their designated mounting area, Mary paid very little if any attention at all to the small puddle of clear sticky liquid, with a pinkish nucleus, on the flooring of the elevator, just behind where she stood.

She was holding the hand of her toddler son in what she called a mother's protective grip. As the elevator began to rise to the next level, the woman ruffled her young toddler's hair, before she knelt down on one knee to adjust his collar and wipe the sleep from his small eyes. Once they'd reached the top floor, she once again took the toddler's hand, proceeding into the upper concourse. They arrived at the gate with only a few minutes to spare and as soon as she showed the nice lady at the desk their boarding passes and her passport, she kindly informed her the flight to Paris was now ready to embark.

The announcer mentioned that she and her boy were welcome to proceed through the gateway, as she was about to make the first on board announcement. Mary was giddy at the prospect of leaving the U.S. for the very first time. But she was also scared almost to the point of nausea, as this would be her first time ever stepping foot on a plane. Her toddler's father, though not her husband, had been an excellent dad and terrific supporter to them both, since he'd learned of her conception. She had been the one who did not believe that their friendship should become anything more than just that throughout his overseas contract. But it was he, who insisted that she should at least come to France, as soon as she and the baby were physically able to fly. In fact, he had surprised her for Christmas with first class tickets for her and their son to encounter Paris to see how she liked it. She fought him lovingly, tooth and nail about making the move to the French Capitol permanently. "Are you OK little buddy?" she asked. More for her sake than his own as she took her first steps across the threshold of the jumbo 747 transatlantic air craft.

"Welcome aboard Trans-Air flight 143 to Paris France Madam, will this be your first time flying with us?" the fairly pretty woman in the too tight white blouse, too short blue skirt and too loud lipstick asked, as she personally lead the two of them to their plush, first class accommodations. She had only a brief minute to take in the enormity of the jet before her and her young man were tucked safely into their lavish leather seats. They were given blankets, and ear phones for the TV and in-house movies that would be shown over the duration of what would be an almost eleven hour flight. Reaching for the window covering, she slid it up half way, and peered out like a frightened little girl, realizing for the first time how far she was from the ground already and how close she was to the outside of the aircraft. At that moment she crinkled her nose sharply and made a face. "Uh Oh, did someone make a Mr. Stinky or did that view just scare a Mr. Stinky out of Mommy?" she asked. The toddler laughed, shook his head and said, "No Mommy, I didn't make Mr. Stinky."

To be on the safe side she asked the brightly colored stewardess for directions to the lavoratory and once again the lady made it her mission to escort them directly to the door of the closest family bathroom facility to her first class section of the aircraft. Once they'd gotten into the astonishingly spacious restroom, she was pleased to find that, true to his word his disposable diaper was still totally dry. "That's Momma's good boy!" she yelped as she ruffled his hair and sat him on the small toilet seat. "Now could you try to go titi for Momma before we get going? I bet you I can recover a cookie in my bag somewhere if you do. The child smiled proudly as the sound of titi trickled into the bowl below him.

Once the trickle had stopped she took a wet-wipe from a plastic sleeve in her inside blazer pocket. She then noticed the weird gray-green tint to the water, but figured it was probably only some chemical that they used in the bathrooms to keep them smelling fresh and clean during the duration of the long overseas flights. She quickly redressed him and the two of them stepped out of the bathroom just in time to come face to face with the plane's co-pilot. "Hello there future navigator" he said, basically in fun before he promptly disappeared into the rest room for his last chance to relieve himself before final departure.

The Marine Patrol along with the U.S. Navy and Coast Guard had just about searched every shore affected by the blast radius on lock down. What they found the next morning had assured them that it had been for a good reason. One of the Marine Patrol officers, patrolling the beach on an ATV had come across what he had first thought to be a massive jelly fish in an even larger cluster of seaweed. What he realized right away was that what he is staring at was something historic. Jellyfish didn't have webbed fingers or a large bulging eye. Even though, a lot like whatever this was seemed to have bio-fluorescent skin, there was no doubt in his mind that jellyfish didn't have teeth. He thought about poking it with a stick but thought better of it when he observed the light reflecting off of the object signified that it had moved. "Nobody is ever going to believe this" he told himself before he'd even imagined calling it in. But he stood now with cell phone in hand, pointed at this thing, ready to snap off an impression to download to his Facebook page. The young patrol officer took the first photograph and noticed that it only appeared to be a dark lump and was glad that his new Hi-Tec cell came with a flashbulb feature for its camera. He snapped off a second image and the flash caused the picture to glare due to the things fluorescent skin. He could easily make out the form and would be more than happy to explain clearly that it was neither fish nor human. Feeling a somewhat bolder now, he leaned in a little closer with his camera to what had looked like a huge eye and took another photo.

The camera's flash directed brightness into the things eye and caused it to scream out in a sound like the young patrol had never heard in his lifetime. The man wanted at this point to turn and run back toward his ATV. To grab his receiver and call this in, but he now found himself unable to move. He was seemingly sinking into the earth as if it were quicksand. The man reached down, expecting to use his hands to help push himself up out of the sand that seemed to quickly suck him under. But as soon as his digits touched what he thought was the ground, they too had begun to dissolve away, painlessly, in much the same manner that his legs had done.

The man scanned on in disbelief as his fingers literally dripped off, right before his very own eyes. It was then that he watched in utter horror as the massive round orbs began to glow a radiant blue-green. They appeared to shine more brilliantly as they got closer. The only thing that he could think about was that he had never seen such a beautiful blue in all his life and how he would definitely take pictures if he'd still had fingers. As the being slithered toward him, he looked back to his ATV one final time. Just at that moment he saw the red light on the two way radio illuminate, which let him know that there was a message coming in. Excitement instantly took over; causing his adrenalin to rush, as well as the decomposition of what had been his flesh.

"Unit two we're going to check further up toward Rooster's Rock. If you happen to come across anything, don't hesitate to hit us up as we will be keeping the lines of communications op. . ."The sound ended along with the radio as the iridescent substance began to consume the ATV, the tuner and what was remaining of the young male on patrol. The last words that he uttered before his face was liquefied as well were, "I really would have thought that this would have hurt like hell, but I don't feel a thing." Inside a matter of seconds, he and his ATV had also become one and literally dissolved into the sand like the incoming tide, leaving only the clump of seaweed. After not acquiring a response to their receiver for him, the others U-Turned and headed back to the perimeter that they left the youth patrolling. They searched for three miles beyond the range that they had given him to search. After finding no trace of either him or his ATV and still getting no answer by wireless, they had no choice but to call it in to local police as a person now gone missing. Within hours of sunset all remnants disintegrated into the sand.

The Sharply dressed cop stepped out of the rest room looking every bit the part of an officer and a gentleman. He immediately caught the eyes of both female and male passengers as he sauntered through first class, headed toward the plane's cockpit, where he'd spend the next eight to ten hours in flight.

As he made his way through the first rate area of the aircraft, the police stopped briefly to acknowledge a lady with a toddler, seated in the 1st class section. "Good morning future pilot" he said to the youngster as he approached the two of them. The boy's mother smiled sheepishly at the dapper young wing man as he tipped his hat to her in passing. The gentleman quickly disappears through the cockpit door, locking it as it closed behind him. "The officer sitting in the captain's chair looked over at him almost as if he had seen a ghost. "Jay Striker, you made it; I was told that you'd been scratched from this morning's roster as a no show."

The captain and number one navigator said to his newly arriving co-pilot. "Well here I am, in the flesh and in living color. So what you see is what we got," the chief stated before the two men broke into simultaneous laughter. Mary and her toddler got situated for the long overseas flight. Other commuters boarded the plane, making their way to their assigned seats, some on this level and others on the upper floor. All passengers and crew were loaded with no incident and taxing and take off all went without a hitch. In fact, Mary had gotten so comfortable, that soon after her boy closed his eyes and rested, the sheer silence lulled her right off to a deep, dreamless sleep. When she awakened she felt more in a dream than when she had actually been asleep. She knew that the little guy strapped in next to her was her son. But he now looked much more grown up than when she had dozed off, just a short time ago.

A quick glance at her watch reassured her that she had slept no longer than forty minutes. Yet here he was in his small Oshkosh jeans, his legs now protruding a full three inches out of the bottom. At some point he must have taken his own shoes off, as they lay untied and sitting next to feet that could not fit in them if they had been forced. She stared at him almost in panic strikingly, before reaching out to touch his forehead and ask yet again, "Are you OK little buddy." He looked her straight in the eye; his own eyes now looking greener than even she remembered and said, "I can really go for a bite to eat" he'd annunciated clearly. Clearer in fact than she had ever heard him speak in her life. She fumbled through his diaper bag, and pulled out a bottle, but due to regulations, no liquids were allowed on the aircraft. At this moment she summoned a flight attendant and asked her for lukewarm water for the baby's milk.

Within minutes the stewardess returned with one cup of hot fluid and another of cold, placing them both into the outstretched hands of the anxiously waiting mom. She currently mixed the two together in his bottle, already containing the pre-measured amount of formula. Sealed it up and shook it fiercely with one hand while holding onto the nipple of the bottle with the other.

Once this task had been completed she squeezed the bottle and sprayed some of the formula upon the back of her hand to check the bottle's temperature. Then she placed it to her lips, just as she always did, to make sure that the taste was to her approval.

Squeezing the teat gently between her fingers, she caused the warm liquid to now squirt across her tongue and down her throat. In of a few seconds of swallowing, her neck seemed to dissolve from the inside out, causing her to instantly lose any ability to scream. She scuffled momentarily before forming a puddle on the floor just in front of her seat. The thick pool of goo on the carpet shortly made its way behind the leg of the plush chair. It maneuvered around first then between the seating. Right away it reformed itself to look precisely as the form that it had been only a short time before. The hostess asked in passing if the water had suited her purpose, the lady only nodded her head in reply. The operating room in the Bloomfield hospital hadn't buzzed like this in memory. Attendants scrambled to get more supplies as the adolescent mother continued to fight with medical technicians. Even after being given the highest possible dosages of pain killer that they could give a young pregnant teen, and a spinal epidural. Her crying soon started as low squeals to loud and almost ancient screeches. Several large men struggled to somehow bind her to the surgical table, something not normally done during infant deliveries. This in no way appeared to be the standard delivery, and the picture on the sonogram presently showed that this was no average baby. Everyone's glare were now locked on the small monitoring screen, where a three dimensional horror movie seemed to be playing out right before the surgeon's very own eyes. The baby's Mother had finally been restrained with another, even stronger dose of anesthesia. The doctors agreed that it shouldn't affect the nerve center of the child at all. Especially since it had already eaten through its umbilical cord and now seemed to be growing larger before there very eyes. The young girl's tummy immediately became obscenely extended and deformed. The decision was made to cut. The scalpel had but touched the purple, pre-marked area on the girl's abdomen, when it ruptured. Not diagonally as the line and the direction had suggested, her stomach had split horizontally, from spine to spine on both sides. Had anyone noticed, they might have thought that the girls belly looked as if it had been completely and cleanly breached by some giant guillotine. What the people were now paying attention to was a baby, at the moment, climbing down off of the delivery table. It was just born, by its own power and gripping a long tattered piece of his mother's entrails as he climbed nakedly down to the floor. The medical staff all but froze in place as the infant stood calmly and quietly in the middle of the room, taking each of them in. The newborn gazed up at a pretty East Indian intern who had now actually begun to sweat right through her surgical mask.

It offered her a big toothy smile of jagged and crooked teeth, before then offering her a sampling of his mother's own bowels. The woman fainted flat out, a reaction that seemingly startled the newborn, which then stepped back and offered the section of his mother's innards to the next available person. The baby was changing into something else, not human. After nobody took it up on its offer, the thing sat cross legged on the ground and ate the remnants of the internal organs. It ate what was left of his umbilical cord right down to its navel. The creature stuck a digit fully in until the finger disappeared, pulled it out, and sucked lovingly. This sent two thirds of the residents in the OR scrambling into the hallway. They were trying to attend to their fallen comrades. A forth had removed the big clear pliable top from the incubator.

The medic was now attempting to sneak up on the newborn from behind with the large rigid overlay in front of him. At that instant the huge critter turned on its haunches. Just in time to see the man spring forward, slamming the pliant covering down over it with such a force that a piece of a chipped edge flew completely across the room. His action had not only knocked the varmint onto the floor, but it had also scared the piss out of it. Urine that had caused the edges of the shroud to melt, then to bubble, fume and actually catch fire. At this moment the remaining, conscious occupants of the room made a run for the exit doors. Vapor from the burning plastic cover quickly set off both the smoke alarm and the sprinklers. The sound flooded the room with noise and the sprinkler engulfed it with a very large volume of fluid in a very short time. Due to the rooms drain, there was no chance of the water raising enough to have drowned even the most normal newborn that might have found itself alone on an operating room, in a situation as this, only minutes after birth. The water now swirling towards the drainage grate in the middle of the room looked to be the only thing still holding the creature's attention. Like the condensation, it too slid over to the grating, dissolving through the metal and into the floor.

Still wanting to be absolutely sure that he was doing it right, because he could in no way afford to screw this up, he reached into his bib overalls, took out his Bic lighter and lit it to be sure that the switch said down for on and not up. Lehigh Valley's Department of Zoning and Improvement had long sought after ways to get rid of that trailer park.

It had only taken two and a half hours to totally shut down the city of Atlanta, when an un forecasted snow stranded travelers in their cars for more than twenty-four hours, as I-75 and The Atlanta beltway were brought to a frozen stand still. There were 940 confirmed accidents and two and a half inches of snow and ice that covered highways, bridges and side roads. School kids were forced to house in place, meaning they were kept in the schools because there was just no way for buses or any other traffic to get through.

Frozen roads in Pensacola Florida had good citizens in tank tops pushing a Mazda off of frozen roads when temperatures there hit twenty-two degrees in a matter of hours. The Welcome to Florida sign at the state line as you drove in from the state of Georgia was loaded down with a coat of ice, with icicles and barely visible for the heavy snow fall that was now blanketing a region totally unprepared for snow. Home Improvement stores and grocery stores alike stayed open overnight, to accommodate the masses of stranded motorist.

This scene repeated itself across over two thirds of the United States, each time having the same gridlocking affect. Not once did anyone consider that the troubles that they were facing were not coming from the sky above, but instead from the earth below, where the frozen waters were now rising at an alarming rate, during a record breaking cold snap and this was only just the beginning.

As temperatures continue to drop and the waters continue to rise, so did the chances of a major catastrophe in major cities all over the eastern hemisphere. The airport soon became a giant campground and the beltway around the metro, a giant frozen parking lot. It was no secret that the south was poorly prepared for snow and ice, but truth of the matter was, this had not been caused by record snow fall alone. What was happening now was pure and simple revenge on a global scale. This historic traffic mess was not so much caused by two storm systems having perfectly timed their arrival to where it could have the most cataclysmic affect, but by the man having unknowingly pissed off his closest neighbor at the worst possible time. People did eventually make it home, but when they arrived, those that had basements or any area below ground, had water that was frozen solid inside their home.

"RETALIATION"

The beginning phase was seen as nothing more than an unusually cold season. Sayings like, "a hard winter storm has been long overdue." This was heard as temperatures in the great lake states plummet to as low as twenty below zero for nearly the entire first week of the year. It was being called the deep freeze of the decade. It was as far south as the Florida panhandle. The blizzard caused roads to quickly fill and the heavy mechanisms that helped to raise the massive bridges over

Florida's famed rivers and waterways to malfunction. Gridlock came to the city of Atlanta's Hartsfield -Jackson International. The airport was shut down by blinding snow and the beltway around town soon became a jumbled mess of mechanical mayhem.

"The Polar Vortex" as it was called in the north, had caused record setting temperatures as far south as Alabama. The college students at Tuskegee University were released early to partake in a massive snowball fight. While at the same time Anchorage Alaska was enjoying a seventy-six degree heat wave. Frustrations mounted, as natural gas prices continued to rise but availability began to dwindle, as supplies are quickly diminished. It cost about four hundred dollars to fill the tank to warm even a smaller home through winter. Many had resulted to alternate ways of keeping warm. Some legally, some not so legal, some safe not so safe, some pretty ingenious, and some, for the lack of a better term were just down right stupid. A hillbilly husband from Lehigh

Valley Pennsylvania came up with a plan that might very well have worked, if didn't he have the brains of stink bug, his wife so laughingly stated.

One night the redneck drank the last of his own homemade grain to warm up his own innards. Then he got the idea to steal gasoline from the gas company lot down the street just after midnight. He wanted to fill his own tank, as well as any neighbor that might catch a whiff and return the truck before 3 AM and nobody would be the wiser. Around 1am he jogged the half mile or so to the propane corporate area, scampered over the corner of the fence post to avoid the barbed wire. He made it in and across the dingy lot to the line of guzzlers undetected. The yard was always empty at this time of night. Being that it was a small town, dogs would have barked at every varmint that moved in the darkness and pissed off nearby residents. The guy was more than happy to find the door unlocked and the keys over the visor of the very first vehicle he checked. He quickly cranked the huge ten wheeled mobile, dropped it into gear and drove straight out the gate that he simply realized had been opened all the while. Within a matter of seconds the male had backed the big heavy carriage in between his single wide and his neighbors. Cut the engine and the lights off, figuring in under an hour he'd be back home with his family, warm and toasty for the remainder of winter. He promptly disengaged the hosepipe from the base of the six wheeler. He often watched the delivery driver do this many times before. He then attached the end of the hose to the large gray barrel at the rear of his trailer. He marveled at the fact that they paid these guys so much money to do this and here he could do it in the dark. But they wouldn't offer him a job because you needed to apply online and he didn't have a computer, none the less inner net. The neighbor's trailers were still unlit and the sprinkler was now connected to the tank. All he had to do at this moment was figure out which jimmy to pull to get her done. Not being able to see a damned thing out here in the shadows he felt his way around for the lever just above the hosiery leading to his tanker.

Earl purchased his home in Buckhead, with his late wife Irene, fifty years ago this week. This had been home for him, his wife of forty eight years, God bless her soul. His children were raised here and played here with other youngsters and did what typical families did when they were at home. Now, he is in his early seventies and so far able to maintain his own property plus do side jobs for the neighbors. Earl found himself staring down stairs one day that lead to his basement. He was still having a hard time "wrapping his head around" as he'd often hear his kids say, about the idea of putting a koi pond in the cellar. That had been the first thing that came to mind when he'd opened the door the day before to find icy, murky water all the way up to the second step. Earl at this moment was getting ready to turn on the light and had one hand on the switch by force of habit. Then he looked down into the cold, dark water. He already knew for a fact in his brain that the light just wasn't going to work.

But in Earl's mind he thought, "Oh what the hell", as he allowed his finger to quickly flip the breaker up. The light actually flickered on for the briefest time. Then the bulb exploded quietly away into the dreariness. Not before the old man was absolutely sure he caught sight of something. He noted an existence that swam from the direction of the base of the stairs.

He saw it go toward the brightness, in a brief second before the flint went out.

It left Earl staring now into the almost total blackness. He closed the door, locked it from the inside, and asked himself "who would ever believe me?"

When Earl returned the next day, he trudged a wet dry vac with him that he'd just paid double the price for, because the local Do It Yourself stores were all out of stock. The geezer managed to buy this from a young man on the streets, cash. Now back home with the bulky vacuum and several roles of heavy duty extension cords. The elder is now ready to tackle the massive task ahead. Flashlight already on, Earl opened the door slowly. He was afraid if he drew the knob and pulled, it was going to allow the water to come flowing into his home. He was pleased when no water came rushing in, but Earl was ecstatic when he aimed his light close to the door, and saw no water. He stepped around the door and stood with his torch staring into his water damaged but water free basement. After sliding on a pair of big rubber boots, Earl made his way slowly down the still damp wooden stairs, pulling the huge cleaner down behind him one step at a time. Once he reached the bottom of the stairs, Earl turned on the hoover simply to make sure that he had remembered to plug it in. The noise of the wet vacuum quickly shattered the silence and seemed to reverberate deep into the wet walls.

The old man raised the sprinkler to clear the green slime off of the cellar panes, thus allowing light to instantly pour into the room. Every window Earl cleaned with the sprayer had allowed a little more brightness into the space. All at once he cleared the ground floor windows with the brush nozzle on the wet vacuum. He could at this stage see the job that lay ahead. Mold spores were so far visible in lighted spots on the wall. He is thankful at this moment for his homeowner's protection. Even though he realized they said they would have someone out to assess the damages within twenty four hours, Earl knew that the best way to avoid more water damage was to head it off. That is exactly what he intends to do. His long apparent OCD was not going to make this easy for him. The geezer had presently made a game plan to start in the farthest corner and work his path behind and underneath the stairs. Eventually he was sure his insurance company would have a restoration team already in place. The old guy worked up a sweat in no time, but soon came upon another problem that he hadn't considered before today. The Wet-Vac was at this minute, full to the point of uselessness. Earl stood aghast trying to figure out how to get the now completely filled unit back upstairs to empty it. "Just dump it in the deep sink Leepshin" a familiar sound was heard from the dark section of the room. Having perceived that notable voice hundreds of times in this very basement, Earl called out questioningly.

"Irene? Holy kablimises Irene is that you?" "Yes Leepshin it's me. Why are you worried now about dirtying up that old deep sink? It's all going to need a thorough scrubbing with some lye soap when you're done." Earl swallowed hard, hearing that voice which has been silenced only a short time ago. He pressed his hand into his chest, not because he was in pain but to make sure his heart was still actually beating. "You shouldn't be here Irene, this place is a mess. Besides I buried you two years ago, put you away nice, rest in peace and all that good stuff. What on earth are you doing back here?"

"If you don't want me here I'll leave," she uttered in what Earl thought was the most pitiful tone he'd heard from her in all their years together. "Well since it's all about what I want, I want one of those hugs that you always gave me at the end of the day. I want you to hold me and never withdraw from me. I want to hear you say that I'm still the love of your life. That you, to this day adore me and only me." Irene stepped slowly out of the darkness. Not in the pretty cream colored dress that he had put her away so nicely in, but in her favorite floral house coat. She seemed to almost float, as she came across the room to meet him.

She looked as beautiful now as she had when he'd first laid eyes on her fifty-five years ago. Within a matter of seconds he was once again in the firm embrace of the woman that he'd loved for some many years. "Please, don't let go" he voiced, inhaling deeply as if to take in the very essence of her. "I won't ever release you," she said and didn't.

FEBRUARY 4TH

Seventeen water districts in California were now inside of 100 days of drying out.

The San Joaquin Valley is dwelling to more than 40% of the nation's fruit, but due to a severe dry spell in Fresno and surrounding areas. The drought in this area has literally desiccated. Spawning trails for salmon programed to leave the Pacific Ocean and swim upstream to lay their eggs year after year. But now the streams had dried and the access from the oceans remained nothing more than an arid, rocky outcropping. With salmon facing possible extinction and produce prices threatening to more than quadruple, individuals along the east coast are more concerned with their team bringing home the Vice Lombardi trophy, after winning the Super Bowl than the fact that their region hadn't gotten more than an inch of rain in the past year. People used everything from one man kayaks, all the way up to huge speed boats coasting upward of a million dollars to pack Lake Havasu with men and women looking to, kick back, relax, tan, drink and party. Though thousands of partying revelers packed the inlets and its numerous coves and harbors, no one seemed to notice that there was something different about the water. If anything it was even more soothing than many had remembered. Arrest numbers were typical and disturbances were if nothing else, expected.

Even the brave souls that returned for yet another year to cast their bodies, drunkenly out over the water via a knotted hemp rope. Some bold and probably intoxicated idiot had literally gone out on a limb and tied that line out there, who knows how many years ago. Nevertheless drunks bet their bottom dollars and battled booze intoxication trying to see who could fling their drunken body the furthest out into the lake.

Although thousands visited the reservoir daily, the scatterings of Jiffy- Johns were regularly checked, but found to be rarely used. It left park officials to wonder if maybe the vast majority were either pooping on their boats, or holding it until they had departed the lake's immediate area.

As of yet, no feces was reportedly washed up on shore. Rangers even confronted male party goers wearing adult diapers. After taking information from the mens ID, the officers swore to give them both tickets, with fines totaling far more than a flight home if any part of those briefs were found later floating in the lake.

But everyone on the cove wasn't there to get drunk; some were there to get lucky as well. The human sperm count in the river on any given day could total a half gallon minimum. On a busy afternoon or during a holiday weekend, had anyone ever taken account, might have easily filled a five gallon jug.

This once stringy mess is served for nothing more than forming mystical strings of minnow food. It fluoresced in the night waters and became a prized element to the underlings. They were now finding ways to capture and store the pearly essence in empty plastic bottles. Carafes easily found along the many coasts and beaches that mankind has inhabited and infected with his own desires to exist. At this rate they didn't even have to leave the safety of home to collect the much needed semen that they so badly needed to achieve species dominance. Once this is done they would simply restore earth to its natural beauty. Mountainous caves and caverns inland and tropical oasis all around, the way God had meant for it to be; the state it had been in the beginning.

The problem was that the day that Eve had been tempted by the serpent to eat of the fruit of the tree of life, they realized their own nakedness. For thousands of years they have built, to cover themselves and their beloved families and things that they hold dear. They never wanted to give any thought to the wreckage, the pollution and the changes that were caused on the earth. The Underlings now had what they needed to rise up and save the planet where they were born and raised from the ground dwellers currently leaving trails of destruction.

Richard was seated in the rear of The Rusty Anchor, not drinking, simply watching. One by one the women connected with an unassuming male, hoping for the times of their life, in all respect like the guys that he worked with and so often came here with. Everyone appeared to be getting attention accept the shorter lady, the one with the deformed lip. It was at this point that a pretty young waitress sauntered over to where he was sitting and asked Richard what he wanted to drink. Richard told her he was fine with what he had, while holding up a half filled glass of cola that had been here since he first arrived. "No charge to you my pleasant man, someone decided you looked good enough to skimp on I guess," she mentioned as she stood, notepad and pen in hand. "I'll just have another soda then, thanks," Rich said to the server who quickly walked away to acquire his fizz.

He scanned again to the group of six, this time his eyes locked with the short woman with the split lip and he mouthed the words thank you. Her mouth opened as if to repeat what he stated but what transpired out seemed to Richard more like waves of light than sound. Still he felt he understood her. But right at that moment her entire entourage gets up and starts toward the front door with several men in tow.

Richard scrambles to put on his coat so that he can follow them out into the cold February night without, trying to seem inconspicuous yet rushing just the same.

As he makes his way through the hoard of happy hour hopefuls, Rich finally reaches the exit in time to see the six women and their five male companions, all go into different directions in the parking lot. Richard decided to walk behind the shorter one, now alone and nearing the end of the parking lot. The irony was that there were no vehicles parked that far out, only the high wall where the parking lot dropped into the waters below. Richard continued to follow at a distance, as she seemingly walks right off of the edge of the almost twenty foot drop off onto the massive boulders below. Thinking this a possible suicidal jester, if not a cry for help, Richard ran quickly now toward the jetty. He peered over, only to find nothing there but the stones that lined the city's spillway, and the bulky drain pipes that permitted the rain to flow from the city out here into the city's huge drainage channel. Much to his surprise there was no one there on or near the rocks. The water levels were low, so it wasn't like she would have been washed away by currents. Due to the cities lack of precipitation you could have quite easily walked completely across the concrete aqueduct without getting much more than your socks wet. Seeing no one on the rocks or in the area beyond the seawall, Richard looked behind him once again. He allowed his eyes to once again do a quick scan of the lot.

Noticing nobody there and seeing no way that the woman could have doubled around and got past him, Richard climbed over the seawall. He scaled down onto the boulders with his back against the stone wall while his eyes regulated to the blackness. In a matter of minutes, Rich maneuvered his way along the wall toward the lower edges of the parking lot. On the other side of the fence, arriving to a location where he visited many times over the previous few decades. Rich now stood in a spot that until right now he had no idea existed. Once he had rounded the fifteen foot structure, he came upon something that made all the sense in the world, but had never been considered. Below the city ran enormous brick pipes, probably hundreds of years old. There were pipes that formed a massive network of interconnecting pipelines that drew water from the streets of the city out into the reservoir. Only after his eyes had adjusted to the darkness did he notice the huge eight feet, red cinder pipe that disappeared deep into the cities under belly.

Still, with no sight of her, Richard starts to question his sanity and why he had come down here below the seawall in the first place. As he turns to make his way back to the spot where he had climbed down from the parking lot, a slip of the foot caused several loose bricks to fall away. In turn it had led something to run scampering deep into the pipe, splashing loudly as it made its way far into the tube.

New Jersey dodged a bullet by only about five hours after hosting the Super Bowl in Met Life Stadium. Fans trying to get home by commuter rail, bus and other forms of public transportation are pelted with another heavy round of snow, compliments of winter storm Maximus. This is one of many storms to pulverize the entire territory during the blizzard of 2014. It was only a few days that past from storm Maximus to storm Nika. This is at a time when propane that should have been available had been shipped out to one country or other as part of some foreign stimulus package. The gas tanks that remained were in great command, and we all know that demand drives up prices.

The cost of heating oil was climbing as quickly as the icy waters were now elevating and the temperatures were dropping. As frozen water, deep in the surface of the globe gets forced upward toward the top; something else extraordinary begins to take place. Trees, some with roots that have stretched as far into the ground as their limbs have reached into the sky. They are now being pushed up out of the foundation by the phenomenon that was now taking a position just below the surface. Trees that seemed nearly as old as time, now appeared to be giving up their ghost, rising and then falling.

Tree limbs and hefty branches, coated in thick sheets of ice; literally explode as they shatter under the weight of the sleet and snow, bringing thousands of limbs down on hundreds of power lines. More and more roads soon became impassable as tree after tree rose and then fell onto the frozen earth below. Humans, who once felt so safe in their dwellings, now scampered and scurried to find any way at all to keep them and their families warm. A mission that had proven daunting in the beginning and virtually impossible as days drew on into winter. Salt trucks by the thousands, manned the thruways and byways of major cities attempting to maintain the freeways clear for the sake of commerce. Electrical contractors from near and far were stretched to their tear point trying to remain with demands to restore energy, in what seemed to them like some of the most isolated places on earth.

Vehicles stranded in snow drifts along main parkways across the country, turned out to be extra added barriers and barricades. Even massive salt trucks, so heavily depended on to provide layers of protection on the highways from the heavy snow, are now reportedly becoming victim to the sleet themselves as they too now begin sliding and toppling over into ditches. People were starting to resort to extreme measures in a not simple battle to retain heat.

A swine farmer, fearing the worst and facing the possibility of losing all of his prized pork, had made the drastic decision to move his family into the barn for the duration of season. He could no longer afford to maintain both his home and his pigs cozy. The temperature in the farmer's home was usually kept at sixty-five during the winter. The shed was maintained at sixty-eight, because a cold pig is a thin pig. Seeing no other option, the rancher moved his wife and children in amongst the beast of the field. Others hadn't faired as luckily, as propane rapidly ran out and access routes to them quickly iced over. Back to back snow and ice storms in the mid-west and northeast caused a lot snow days for schools. As well as record calls to 911 and most visits to emergency rooms, some had come simply in hopes of keeping warm.

One man, after completely running out of gas and the ability to keep his household heated, brought his bar-b-que grill into the living room. Loaded it down with charcoal, lighter fluid and set his residence on fire, burning it entirely to the ground within a matter of minutes. Watching his house and all of its possessions go up in flame should have been the most painful thing on earth to witness. But the peasant and his brood now did what many, before this present time, might have thought to be a sign of someone having totally lost their mental faculties.

Neither the man, nor any of his family members made any attempt to put out the blaze that had now completely gutted the structure that they until now called home. Instead they scampered to and fro, trying to find dry wood to throw into the fire to keep the warm flame burning for as long as was humanly possible.

A state of emergency was declared in over eighty percent of the U.S. as calls for urgent assistance began to only go unanswered. There was very little the state or government officials could do to head off the barrage of disappointing news looming on the horizon. Everyone had to wait and wonder simply how bad things would get. While ice and snow blanketed two thirds of the United States, the western hemisphere is suffering from record drought conditions. Some areas water levels are so low that fish had been left stranded in puddles that used to be creeks and rivers.

After what had turned out to be a very active fire season along California's San Bernardino mountain ranges, brothers Travis and Jason were merely glad to be finally getting a much needed vacation. Even though the boys were born only minutes apart, Travis always claimed that he was a year older than his sibling because Travis had been born on December 31, 1982 at 11:58 PM. His brother had arrived only seven short minutes later at 12:05 AM but in the following year.

This was often a bone of contention between the brothers, but hardly anything else in life had been. The duos have been inseparable from birth. Raised in La Quinta California, they both pursued careers with the forestry service as firemen. They both manage to be recruited to the same squad after they'd both past every type of agility test and completed the battery of book work required of them with some of the highest joint scores on record in the history of their battalion. Coming up the two had fought all of their battles together, even when they'd brawl each other. Any other that decides to challenge either one of them would have been dealt with harshly by the both of them. Both men had grown up to be ruggedly handsome, with that lumberjack mannerism that just seemed to make the valley girls long for the hills.

Jason, being the quieter of the two, would spend hours and days, taking anything electronic or electric apart, only to rebuild it even better than it was before Once, while their team had been fighting a range fire in steep mountainous terrain, they came across a young couple who had been camping and got lost in the San Jacinto Mountains with no cell phone signal. In a matter of seconds, Jason transformed their inoperable wireless to a transmitter that set off an emergency beacon which lead air search and rescue to their exact location within half an hour's time.

The boys worked hard and they also played hard as well. They could often be seen either blazing through the Ocotillo Wells Vehicular recreation area on ATV's or homemade Dune Buggies. You simply might find the two of them thundering across the Salten Sea on fast powered jet skis that Jason rigged to speed and turn tighter than any other water craft of its kind. Two preteen boys, angling off of Capri lane in Desert Shores, along the lake's south-western shore, watched as the two jet skis screamed off toward the other side of the cove. Each marveled at how far the plumes shot up from behind the two water propelled rockets, as they jetted further away by the second. Both fishing wire bounced simultaneously and the boys totally forgot all about the two jet skis, in anticipation of a bite. Without sound or warning noise, the high streams of water and the jet skis were gone.

To the boys, it barely looked as if they may have been overtaken by a wave, had they been looking, but something big was now on both their lines. The boys laughed giddily as they fought like fishermen to hall in their catch. The older boy seemed to be having a much harder time at landing his cast, but both managed to stay in the fight until whatever it was, was narrowly out of sight in the river before them.

One final pull and the boys were both covered with water and then just gone. Now once again the lake was still, except for the tiny wake caused by the jet skis when they'd first passed the boys on their way across the reservoir. Even the boy's bicycles and tackle boxes had been devoured by what had looked like a rogue ripple. Not a wave that traveled quickly across the water's surface, but one that simply rose up from the water's edge that devoured everything in sight. As the wave dissolved into the sand, so did the teen bikes and fishing tackle.

FEBRUARY 7TH

One month and seven days into the New Year, conditions caused all the oceans of the earth to rise and connect, becoming one body of water. For the first time since the continents had divided, thousands of years ago, salt, fresh and brackish waters now all mixed substantially enough to where all the earth's ponds, lakes, rivers, reservoirs, tributaries and estuaries entirely shared the same brilliant emerald green color. The water was dead calm and the surroundings were perfect for recovery efforts to resume for the ill-fated flight of a 747 jumbo transatlantic air craft. Trans-Air flight 143 to Paris France lost radio contact only a few hours after leaving the east coast and were never heard from again. The military was trying to triangulate vectors to try and kind of figure out approximately where the plane should have been.

Then they looked for evidence such as an oil or fuel slick on the water or visible wreckage along the airplanes approximated flight path. The coastguard cutter Lawrence followed the plane's suggested course, but crew members had not only reported no visual sign of any destruction or fuel spill but their sonar had also showed nothing on the sea floor below them either. Although the human calculations put the aircraft's whereabouts in this general vicinity, give or take a hundred square nautical miles, this direction or that. There had been no distress calls received by the jumbo aircraft, it had simply disappeared at sea. The first alarms in the cockpit of Trans-Air flight 143 to Paris France warned that the plane was reaching dangerously low altitude. The second was a stall warning, indicating that the plane's speed had become too slow to keep its massive weight in the air.

The passengers had all been strapped in and looked to be asleep. Both levels of the jumbo jet were quiet and lights had long ago been dimmed. It was near midnight back on the east coast and soon to be dawn in Paris. The commander had taken the watch after the Captain set and locked the auto pilot. The navigator appeared to sleep quietly as the co-pilot, whom he had worked with on Trans-Atlantic crossings many times, now unlocked the auto pilot on both sides. He lowered the air craft to less than one hundred feet above the sea. The very first alarm sounded only seconds before the stall indicator informed the cockpit that the plane was about to fall out of the air.

It was at the moment that the co-pilot turned on all of the planes forward landing lights, shining the Ocean, only depths below them. As the light materialized and unrolled upon the water, the water seemed to spread out in front of the plane; in fact the water was actually parting. From wing tip to wing tip, the plane descended. Its wings were presently at water level. The massive engines and quite possibly the wings would have been torn off by the pressure of their impact with the ocean, were the ocean not at this minute moving out of its way. Ahead of the aircraft was a great abyss, a drop off into what looked like a total void. With the exception of a large trench in the side of the continental shelf, the co-pilot guided the jet directly into the hole. The waters now closed up in the briny around and above them. There was no tail oil or fuel spill on the surface to glisten in the early morning sunlight. No crash debris to signify the location of collision. There was only a drunken sea captain, high on drugs and alcohol and down on his luck, trying to make out some form of existence at sea by hiding in the deep behind the assumption that he's a fisherman.

Truth be told, he has ripped off more people than he'd cared to remember. So many in fact that there was someone in every continent, not necessarily waiting to, but wanting to and looking forward to killing him. What he just witnessed could fix all of his problems and leave him set for life. But who was going to consider that he'd watched the ocean totally opened up and quietly swallow a 747. Then it closed up again without the wake ever rocking his boat; He didn't even believe it.

The vast accumulation of snow across the country gave caused for a massive melt down. Then all of a sudden, for no reason at all, after nearly a month of temperatures below thirty and weeks of days and nights below freezing, the sun allowed a day that went up to 82 degrees. Thousands of snow and cold dreary northerners welcomed the chance to give up boots and heavy coats for flip flops and jean shorts. The water however, being twice as warm as the land masses around it, seemed to smoke as it almost steamed its way through mountains and valleys.

The strange occurrence momentarily spawned its own Eco system, as the warm mist surged from the watercourse and rivers. It began to rise, not as steam but as a thick warm fog. It rose quickly into the cool air, only to form rain clouds only a few feet about the mountain tops. The run off from the quick thaw of layers upon layers and miles and miles of snow covered peaks, had generated brooks to not only flood their banks, but to carve deep gashes in the earth. Thus forming new creeks, streams and tributaries, of which in time made their way back to one sea or another eventually.

Within a matter of days, eighty percent of major roads across the U.S. had suffered considerable damage from erosion and many had been totally washed out altogether.

Mud washed some homes off of their foundations while others were swallowed up by rivers that had now overflowed their banks, some by miles. All over the country, temperatures rise, as trees, bridges and power lines came down. Basements and yards all across the northeast flooded, leaving people to maneuver by boat and even by Jet Ski to get around. Then, as quickly and as quietly as the warm spell had snuck in, causing massive flooding from Main to Montana, another Canadian clipper system swooped down out of the northwest. It caused temperatures to suddenly drop to well below freezing for weeks to come. The Susquehanna River had overflowed its banks for miles on both sides from Sunbury Pa. It first took over 11 and 15, and washed out almost every road, home, bridge, vehicle and human in its path all the way through the small mountain side town of Duncannon. Then it demolished the entire township down river into Marysville and Enola before the rubbish finally began to pile up against the many overpasses that separated the capital city of Harrisburg from the smaller cities on the western shore of the now grotesquely swollen Susquehanna.

It was then that the arctic blast had struck, bringing wintertime back with a vengeance and freezing almost all items in its tracks. In this case, everything in its path included over one hundred twenty six winter weary men, women and children who now wanted nothing more than for this cold season to be over so that they could once again get out and spend time with family and friends. Little did anyone know it then, but normal as we'd come to know it made a few differences. Many more changes would take place in the days arriving. Heating oil prices had already reached record highs in the weeks ahead of this storm. But now the rush of water and massive over flow had over taken the Three Mile Island Hydro Nuclear Power Plant, in Londonderry Township, Dauphin County Pa.

It caused an emergency shut down after the warm water had first risen to registered heights. Flooding overflows had then refrozen solid within a matter of days afterwards, stopping turbines. While flood waters were still almost a foot in depth along major truck routes like the Pennsylvania Turnpike and along Interstate 83, vital thoroughfares for traffic headed in and out of Pennsylvania by way of Maryland. Omaha to Ocean Side Maryland were now beneath a deep hard freeze. Thousands upon thousands of people from Michigan to Main now found themselves literally living in frozen tundra. They had little if any hope of urgent help getting to them any time soon.

There was more than a third of the United States now under a winter weather emergency conditions. It was currently unreachable by federal crisis management officials. A quarter of the now remaining populations were women, children or senior citizens. There were a few enduring males that were still healthy but were stretched thin trying to do whatever they could to help. Septic tanks had long frozen and backed up. Sewer lines sat filling, but with nothing for sewage to do but build up, which again caused toilets to back up. People were throwing buckets of raw solid waste out their rear door and collecting pails of snow out front, to use for everything from cooking to bathing and using the toilet. One ice storm had paralyzed the city of Atlanta Georgia. Two winter storms had crippled the nation. A third ice storm, a nor'easter named Paxton brought sleet and freezing rain into Atlanta, canceling twelve hundred flights in and out of Hartsfield – Jackson Atlanta International Airport alone.

The storm barreled north along the east coast. It pulled moisture first from the Gulf of Mexico and then from the Atlantic Ocean as it set its sights on shutting down not just Atlanta this time but the entire northeast.

There were over one hundred and eleven thousand customers without power in the beginning of the snowstorm in Georgia. Nearly thirty thousand residents in the state of South Carolina were already with no energy when the storm hit. The chances of a good outcome looked bleak. Many northerners were accustomed to harsh winter conditions. They knew that even if they lost electricity that their local electrically operated companies would have their electric reimposed, in a matter of days. Surprisingly in the very worst case scenario, it would only take a matter of weeks. But this blizzard would be different. Major freeways having overpasses that have corroded or iced over and most minor streets were now blocked by fallen shrubs and washed out aqueducts. Commerce had quickly grown to a halt. Huge power outages meant gasoline stations were closed, for hundreds of miles, as fuel pumps worked by current were out of order. Cars with means soon found lanes impassable.

It was either due to eroded roads or bridges, downed trees or by other vehicles that had become stranded in icy surroundings or had simply run out of gas or diesel. Volunteer firemen in outlying areas find themselves trying to fight the flames with water that froze the second it cleared the tubes, literally spraying home fires with icicles. The mere task of re-rolling up the massive, frozen hoses to be restored on the truck had itself turned into a back breaking job.

The storm left hundreds dead or dying from Louisiana to Canada. With reasons that ranged from drowning, to freezing, to house or vehicle fire, to electrocution, after one man tried to electrically heat the water in his home, with deadly results.

By spring 178,242 people had been confirmed gone in the eastern United States, another sixty-two thousand were unaccounted for, some reported missing, all assumed done for. For the first time in anyone's memory, waves of ice on the quickly rising Atlantic Ocean, over took coasts. Beating an extended, and quite thunderous, icy percussion against sea walls and board walks from Myrtle Beach South Carolina to the glorified lobster lodgings of Gloucester Main. Many along the Jersey seaboard had just returned after rebuilding from the summer hurricane that had destroyed most of the Jersey shore and Atlantic City's boardwalk. Only to have it burn up soon after reopening from a fire. Now they watched in horror as frozen tides ate away at private waterfronts, growing closer each hour to their beloved sanctuaries. Ones they thought sank every dime of not only their own, but their kid's inheritance as well.

By Thursday evening, the icy waves were lapping hungrily at the seawalls and the sun decks of the multimillion dollar homes. By morning most of the beaches along the east coast looked as if they had been set back in time one hundred years over night.

No house lasted along the shore between Savannah Georgia and Portland Main. On the east coast not one building remained within a mile of the beach. It seemed they had either been washed into the sea or had sunk into the water saturated sands, returning the beaches now to their natural state. Another major snow storm not only devastates but devours most of the eastern seaboard. The whirlwind swallowed up casinos, boardwalks, ocean front businesses, homes and their owners and occupants. Then it raced off of the east coast and into the Atlantic Ocean where an additional strong storm front was moving east across the Pacific Ocean.

The storm had been picked up on National Oceanic and Atmospheric Administration's (NOAA) Doppler radar. It had been determined to be nothing more than a small weather front, sucking moisture needed to maintain energy from warm waters of the Pacific Ocean. It was quickly decided that as soon as the system made landfall in Safford Island California, it would lose its punch and simply fizzle out over the vast Klamath and Redwood National Forest. The blizzard had been greatly under estimated, as weather officials saw it as nothing more than a small storm front. It was definitely destined to die out over the densely wooded national forest of Northern California. Within a matter of minutes, the storm front made land fall. Rain pelted the region so hard that it had looked like a tropical typhoon, only in the far northwest.

The heavy rains quickly over took Klamath Beach, seeming to almost drink up the Coastal Drive and the peninsula that blocked the mouth of the Klamath River for as long as anyone had known it to exist. Ocean water from the pacific now seemed to nearly get sucked into the mouth of the Klamath River. Broadening by not just inches and feet, but by yards and then by miles on either side. As the water continued to rise and rush inland, using the Highway 101 bridge span across the river has totally decimated the Yurok Indian Reservation on the river's southern bank. Then it cut new paths leading south through the Yurok reservation. The river which had once been narrow and winding had within minutes become a raging torrent. The waterway straightened as the runnel became even wider. It persisted south beside the rivers original track. By the time the Klamath River flowed south to Clair Engle Lake the inlet widened by ten miles and had brought with it every timber, tower and tourist in its path.

The many miles of Highway 169 that has long been a highly favored and very scenic route along the winding river and through the Yurok Indian Reservation, were now lost in a maddening rush of trees. Expensive SUVs with expansive mobile homes and tall timbers were at the moment torn from the ground by the torrent. It now continued southeast at a high rate of speed, through Six Rivers National Forest and on deep into Shasta National Forest.

It joined forces with the massive Claire Engle Lake, quickly pushing the lake over its banks, flooding the Whisky town-Shasta-Trinity Recreation area and the many miles of Highway 3 that had run along the once calm Claire Engle Lake. Within hours the waters of Shasta Lake, as well as inside of the whisky town-Shasta-Trinity Recreation area on the east side of the Trinity Mountains, also began to swell its bankside. The combining waters then combined to cut a new trench.

It formed a current and enormous tributary that directly spread from the Forest in the north and then taking joining the Sacramento River to head south. The recent waterway was now more than eighty miles wide. By nightfall, Stockton, Modesto and Fresno were all ocean front cities, but to their west, as the San Andreas Fault almost completely filled with water, mud, cars, trees, expensive SUVs, expansive mobile homes and people.

In Holy Cross City a naturalist had grounded himself first in a steamy flow of the nearly raging water and then in a cavern at the rear of the fall. The almost too hot water was exactly what he had needed to both reinvigorate his body and cleanse both himself and his clothing. Leaning backward in the tepid stream, now almost completely submerged, he had noticed a warm breeze that appeared to be coming from behind the falls. What he had found in the back wall of the waterfall was a cave, lined with large purple rocks, which seemed to light a path deep into the caves underbelly.

The scientist strolled his way deep into the cave. Plucking the large stones from their place on the cave wall and jamming them into the pockets of his tattered army jacket. Not until he had picked every stone, did he realize that he now stood in total darkness, deep in the bowels of this cave. The historian immediately pulled both his hands from his torn blazer and quickly realized that he literally couldn't see his hands before his face. Having what he thought was a brilliant idea, the man reached again into his pocket with both palms, grabbed up a bunch of the minerals in each hand, and held them out in front of him. It worked; the gleam wasn't nearly as bright as it had been. But he could at least now tell the direction that the cave went, even though he wasn't sure which direction he had originally come from. Deciding on the most logical conclusion, that right is always the correct choice, he turned right and headed deeper into the cave. Sounds of water running in the shadows in front of him indicated to him, at least in his mind that he must be coming closer to the river. Of course the flow of the river would take him back to the mouth of the cave. The naturalist continued deeper into the cave, led only by the sound of running water and the hopes of soon getting around to the cave's opening. Then he could make plans to start life anew, probably either in Reno or Vegas, living out the rest of his days in luxury. The eerie greenish radiance just beyond the cave walls ahead of him, assured him that a new life was now only inches away. He began to really run deeper into the murkiness, toward the faint green glow only a few feet in front of him.

What he hadn't seen was the drop off between the two glowing green orbs and his self. The naturalist plummeted head on into the tepid turbulent water. Feeling himself tumbling head over heels beneath the warm strong current, determined to hold his breath until the rushing water spit him back out pretty near where he'd come in. The scientist thought he could feel himself being tossed to and fro by the flow. His eyes flashed open just in time to realize six, bright greenish globes, each paired to another, on either side of him, seemingly holding him as he and they were hurtled over and down into what at first appeared as total blackness and sure death. At least in free fall the ecologist had been able to catch his breath. In doing so he opened his eyes, to find himself now surrounded by what looked to him like thin, bioluminescent and very naked women. Their eyes glowed similar to flashlights in the darkness, and he could tell exactly where each one was looking, simply by the light that their eyes had cast. "All eyes on me," he laughed nervously as each of them broke loose from the huddle and made its way toward him. Its fluorescent skin was so sparse that he was certain he could see the blood pulsing through the creature's veins. As the creature moved in closer, he could finally start to make out the silhouette of the small frame that presently seemed to be floating in his direction at the depths of the dark cave. His fears were suddenly put to rest when it came to within feet of him and he saw cleavage.

"I knew it," he said loudly. "I knew I'd died and gone to heaven, and you're angels, you're all angels, right?" he asked, laughing almost hysterically now as one by one they all moved in nearer to him. He could actually see their organs through their thin fluorescent skin. Fluids streaming through their bodies cast an eerie glow against the rocks. "I'm Tom, he said nervously as they drew in even closer, "and you are?" he inquired. "Hungry" the one closest to him replied, through the most beautiful cleft lip he had ever seen.

THURSDAY FEBRUARY 13

Several people were confirmed dead in Indonesia, after the second volcanic eruption on the island of Java. In as many as 2 weeks, it forced the evacuation of tens of thousands of individuals, as Mount Kelud shot debris and ash twelve miles into the sky on Thursday night. The volcano, located fifty miles south-west of Surabaya, the second largest city, could be heard over one hundred and twenty miles away. Some residents told reporters that, "it sounded like thousands of bombs exploding." Another resident was reported to say, "I thought doomsday was upon us. Women and children were screaming and crying."

At Adisucipto International Airport in Yogyakarta on Friday, Indonesia, workers thoroughly checked over a Citilink airplane. It had been covered by the embers from Mount Kelud, which had impacted closures of seven of the regions airports. Reports say that the seven airports were forced to close due to reduced visibility from volcanic ash in the atmosphere. The danger that the cinder poses to the engines of the air craft could leave thousands of passengers stranded. People living within a 6-mile radius of Kelud had been asked to leave mere hours before the eruption. Ash, sand and rocks continued to rain down on areas as far as ten miles away from the crater of the volcano. Almost three inches of heavy gray embers is left on roads, buildings and vehicles.

Based on verified data, over 76,000 people have been evacuated from five cities surrounding the volcano. About 200,000 were affected. Sparks could still be seen at the volcano's peak long after it erupted. Not so deep below the earth's surface, the system continued to collect and rise across oceans and continents. Density changes resulted in water beneath the surface to fill clusters and cavities of what had probably for millennia been warm pockets of methane. Deposits of crude, led to quick expansions between the earth's crust and its mantel. As the chilly waters came into direct contact with substantial underground lakes of hot lava, the reaction is instantaneous. CH4 gas and steam pushes its way up toward the earth's exterior, in search of release from the astronomical buildup of pressure. It is caused by the rapid and turbulent battle now going on all around the world. Just below the globe's layer, between molting magma and the cold water from the seas.

One man was lost after a massive sinkhole stretched out beneath his bedroom while he slept between jobs. In another case an entire lake and its surrounding trees and brush, were swallowed up in Florida. It left nothing but a large, muddy indentation, where there had been a scenic park setting only hours before. An additional Sink Hole in the middle of The National Corvette Museum in Bowling Green Kentucky ate 8 classic corvettes when it opened up beneath the gallery on Wednesday February 12th. The hole not only destroys hundreds of thousands of dollars' worth of vintage corvettes, but also blocks the cave which was of the many passage ways the underlings used to get from river bed to river bed. The intricate tube like structure of passageways was comparable to the highway systems above.

Only these tubular highways were self-propelled and had never in their history encountered an accident none the less a tragic loss of life. While emergency personnel were busy trying to shore up the remaining building, at least long enough to clear out the excess vintage vehicles and for insurance adjusters to take a report for their claim. The underlings were also busy redirecting their subterranean route and sealing up any evidence that the other one had ever been there, being that they left no tracks and used no tools this was a very quick and seemingly almost effortless task.

Cameras inside the building caught the cave in, but not the repairs that had begun to take place almost instantly. Venice underwater and French vineyards washed out: Now the World has also been hit by flooding as torrential rain batter the continents.

Much of Europe has been submerged as huge downpours pummel the continent. In Venice, tourists could only look on in flooded St Mark's Square as rising system continued to flood their dream vacations. The elevated waters turned the romantic city of Venice into an assault course for its residence and visitors. Authorities closed down snow covered roads and banned riverbank traffic on the Danube River due to strong winds. Vineyards in Langoiran, France, are also plunged underwater. Winemakers simply looked on in horror and agony as years of revenue is literally washed away by the soaring flood waters. Drowning whatever hopes they'd had for any kind of a wine season at all. Over a third of Venice is already under water. An unrelenting wave of rain rushes through Italy, flooding the famed St Mark's Square during what is known as an 'acqua-alta' (high-water) alert in Venice.

Hundreds have been evacuated from homes in Pisa, as the city's Arno River looks set to break its banks. Flood-hit towns braced for fresh deluge of water at high tide as new storm sweeps across the country bringing 70mph winds and heavy rain and snow to some areas. Although the rise in the water level was said to be due to gales and currents, the French department of Finistere has been placed on excessive warning. Forecasters warn of tidal waves and extensive flooding. French departments on the Atlantic seaboard have been on alert for strong waves and risk of submersion the Garonne River in

Bordeaux. Western France has now overflowed its banks and was now washing away hundreds of years of history.

High seas were expected to cause more widespread flooding and disruption along France's Atlantic coast. Winter in Serbia had been exceptionally mild, but over the last week a cold spell and snowstorms swept across parts of central and Eastern Europe. Army and police have evacuated nearly a thousand residents from cars and buses that stayed in a deep freeze in northern Serbia. Emergency officials in Serbia reported that loads of vehicles and a couple of passenger trains remained stranded in the country's north, flat area where strong winds have been piling up snow drifts, cutting off communities and roads.

A State Railway Company said it would evacuate several dozen passengers isolated on the two locomotives going to and from Hungary that were unable to move because of the whitewash on the tracks. A few hundred people still remained stuck in frozen precipitation in Northern Serbia. Heavy snowfall in Bulgaria also left dozens of villages without electricity or water as Romanian authorities declared a "code red" weather warning on Wednesday.

Snow drifts in places are 3.5 meters high (11.5 feet high), prompting authorities to close the main border crossing with Hungary. Parts of Austria have also been badly affected after a meter of snowfall in the last two days, blocked steel rails and covered streets. Railways in the community of Lienz, in Austria, have been blocked after a meter of snow fell in 48 hours. The southern city of Lienz, perched high in the Alps, has been blanketed by snow flurries over the last 24 hours, leaving cars and trains stranded. Whole basins in the mountainous region of Tyrol, where Lienz is situated, have been left cut off after sudden snow storms caused travel chaos. Valleys in the Alpine district have been restricted. Roads are obstructed, while the town of Koetschach, in neighboring Carinthia, is equally suffering with snow reaching head height. There is a mixture of rain and snow forecast for Lienz in the coming days meaning conditions may turn icy.

BY DAILY MAIL REPORTER PUBLISHED: 11:39 EST, 1 FEBRUARY | UPDATED: 13:27 EST, 1 FEBRUARY

The Valentine's Day rush was particularly stressful for Rich and his fellow employees. Due to the heavy amounts of snowfall in the middle of the week and the fact that Valentine's Day was at the end of the workweek. It caused lots of people to wait until the very last minute to shop for that particular something for that someone special.

Of course most people did not really want to go shopping in the first place and opted to simply order flowers online. They would rather pay the extra money for someone else to figure out how to get it to their loved ones in the snow and ice. Rich, now being the senior routes man in the area was expected to not only be able to complete his route, but to answer any and all questions that might have come up during the run of the day by his fellow drivers. By the end of the afternoon, Rich wanted nothing more than to throw back a few cold ones at The Rusty Anchor. He liked to check out the camaraderie and unwind from one of the company's most stressful time outside of the holiday season, which basically ran from October until the New Year. Rich never even made it inside the restaurant.

As soon as he drove into the massive, yet scantly filled car park, the first thing he noticed, were eleven figures making their way toward the edge of the parking lot. They were walking near the same seawall that he'd climbed over the side of only seven short days ago. He backed up into a space on the other end of the turf, but in full view of the targeted area, and sat in his vehicle. He waited with the lights and engine off. Watching, as one after the other, each of the females and their male companions disappeared into the dimly lit corner of the brightly illuminated spot. Rich then stayed behind for a few minutes after the final couple had vanished. Then placed his automobile in drive, and proceeded quietly across the sector, headlights off, in the direction of where he'd just watch them go. Richard got out of his vehicle and walked quickly over to the seawall where he had gone over last week. Once he had climbed over the wall Richard navigated his way along the rock ledge, hidden in the shadows by the jetty. Until he'd come back to the prominent iron grate that blocked entrance to the huge drain pipes that crisscrossed in an intricate maze throughout the city. As he arrived once again at the giant steel gate like contraption, Rich noticed that the massive steel grates were not built to ever be access ports. Instead, the thick rebar had been put through holes drilled through the large pipe, then welded to metal cross bars at the top and bottom of the tubes.

With only about a six inch space between each of the railings, Rich didn't even consider trying to squeeze through. He then stood wondering where the couples that he had precisely watched walk over to this very spot had immediately disappeared too. It was at this point that rich heard movement, just behind him and turned to gaze at the shorter of the women. She was standing very close to him. Her full, sultry lips were presently glistening in the shadows, not far from his own. As dark as it was, Rich thought he could still see a glow in her eyes, as she positioned herself barely inches from him now staring up at him longingly. Startled, Rich did not want to let on that she had scared the bejesus out of him. He simply responded, "You really shouldn't be sneaking up on people that way." She didn't respond verbally. Instead she moved even closer to Richard. Her full, split lip now parted lustfully as her eyes appeared to almost glow in anticipation of where this might possibly lead. Suddenly Rich felt light headed as their eyes locked briefly, the gleam of her eyes seemed to suck him in. Before he had even realized it, Rich tilted his considerably taller frame toward the much shorter woman, granting her total access to his own lips now as well. Instead of touching her lips to Rich's lips, the short female with the fully ripped lip, simply blew into Rich's face. She took him by the hand and led him right through the welded steel opening.

The portals seem to dissolve similar to some kind of cheap magic projection trick, before leading him deep into the tube that would take them into the cities bottomless dark under belly. Rich never even made it into the bar, yet he felt giddy and drunk. It was like back in the teen years when he and the guys would meet out behind the bleachers near the gym to smoke pot after their seemingly daily detention. Even though he had no idea who this woman was, or how they had just gotten through those steel bars, he knew that he was glad to be with her now, here somewhere deep beneath the city.

First off Rich was flabbergasted at how serene it was below ground. A calm had come over him like he'd never felt before, one that told him that he wouldn't mind finding a place down here with this beautiful female and not ever going to the surface again. Turn after turn she lead him deeper and deeper into the bowels or underbelly of the town.

In the almost total blackness Rich found it next to impossible to get any type of bearings. At that time he heard something as familiar as it was out of place, music. Rich could now clearly hear honky tonk music coming from somewhere in front of them. As the musical sounds and singing got louder, he next caught the sound of camaraderie as well, men laughing and having a good old time. The female led Rich around a final corridor, until ahead of them, in the darkness, he could see a door. As the woman pulled him through the doorway, the two of them were instantly bathed in dim light and the resounds of wine, women and song. Rich immediately recognized the setting. It was The Rusty Anchor, yet somehow it wasn't. They had entered through a back door or service entrance that Rich had never taken notice of before. The front entry looked someway different than he'd remembered it looking. But after years and Friday evening Happy Hours spent throwing back beers in the same place, Rich felt pretty sure.

"Hey, Rich is that you?" a familiar voice called from across the room. Over near the far dart board wall, Richard recognized the voice at once and turned promptly on his heels to face the direction of the very familiar voice. "Adam, No way, Adam is that actually you?" The two friends embraced, first like old lovers, cheeks close, hands caressing each other's backs mildly.

Then suddenly, as if both had detected how unmanly this must have looked to the rest of the bar patrons, both men simultaneously slap each other on the back. After they pushed each other away, because they thought it would look like the manlier thing to do. "Where the hell have you been man?" Rich asked sincerely at the same time as Adam had asked him, "So who's your friend Rich?"

They had both attempted to answer in unison, but Richard abruptly realized that he didn't know anything about her, none the less her name. Rich opened his mouth, but remained quiet. "I've been right here drinking free beer," Adam said, holding up a large full frosted mug. "What about work?" Rich asked, now thinking that Adam couldn't have been serious and that somehow this was all a part of a joke and was going to play out here tonight. "Why in the world would I want to go to a workplace when I can get booze, nourishment and any female that I fancy with no charge, in this place, on the house? Speaking of food, you hungry because me and the guys were just about to order some chow, you and your lady come on over and join us." Without another word being uttered, Adam turned and walked back over to two conjoined tables near a front corner of the counter, where Julius, Theo and Sye sat throwing back beers.

"Hey guys, guess who came back," Adam yelled once he'd arrived back at the table. Only skip and Carl were currently missing as the others greeted Rich as though they had only just seen each other at work a few hours ago. "Welcome back buddy, hope you're hungry. This place now serves the best chicken fingers and baby back ribs on the planet," Geo stated before throwing back to back bulls eyes into the dart board. "I personally prefer the meatloaf, Let me tell you," Julius divulged. "The meatloaf here is to die for, No pun intended." "Where are Skip and Carl?" Rich asked as he stood, still in amazement that the guys were actually here. "Skip skipped out," Theo said with a grin. "And Carl got car sick and went for a ride" said Julius between swigs. An extremely thin waitress arrived at their table with two more pitchers of beer, a full slab of baby back ribs and a large side order of the house's special, deep fried fingers. The sauce on the ribs smelled tangy yet sweet. It quickly reminded Rich that he'd had nothing more than a doughnut and a cup of coffee since 4AM. Rich thought the spread was enough to feed all of them twice over. He was about to say so when the server lowered another platter onto the counter. This one was filled with mini sliders, fat little would be hamburgers (had there been bread) on a bed of what looks to Rich like dark seaweed. Julius didn't wait but dug in instantly, devouring the entire round of meat in one quick gulp.

It was not until Julius reached up to wipe the blood like drippings from the corner of his mouth with the back of his hand did Rich even think, It had been Skip who always drooled out of the niche of his lip when he ate. It was also Skip who always drove Julius crazy by wiping his mouth on the back of his wrist, especially during the fall and winter months when they wore uniforms with long sleeve shirts and matching jackets. By the end of the evening, both Skip's uniform shirt and jacket sleeve were covered in spicy sauces. This flashback of memory presently caused Rich to realize that the guys were still in their work clothes.

Rich sat staring at Julius's now stained uniform sleeve and felt an instant urge to void. "I need to take a leak" Rich said, at this moment backing away from the table. "I was just thinking the same thing," Theo said, as he too got up from his place on the far side of the table. "Well hell why don't we all go?" Gio stated as he too rose to his feet. He snatched up a chicken finger, as he too rounded the table to join the others. "Hey Rich, you really gotta try these," Gio shouted as he bit deeply into the large fried digit. 'I didn't realize that chickens even had fingers until this place, they're out of this world." As he sucked every last piece of meat off of the bone and tossed it onto the floor unconcernedly, before the lot of them headed off to the restrooms.

"I never remembered chicken fingers ever having bones in them," Rich said. He followed the rest of them back through the double doors that he and the lady entered through only a few minutes ago. Only this time when they pushed their way through the exit, the back area looked exactly as it had when he and the guys had come here every Friday for the past seven years. There was no sign of the long dark tunnel or the rear entrance that he and the short, beautiful woman with the split lip had used to get in. While the six men took turns sharing the three urinals and the two sinks, Rich found himself realizing at this moment that he hadn't seen the female that he arrived with since he'd gone over to the table.

As the lot of them made their way back out of the men's room, Rich couldn't help but glance over at the pearly digit from the supposed chicken finger, that Gio had so unceremoniously spat against a wall in the hallway as they all headed into the bathroom. Rich also couldn't help but notice how much the discarded bone looked like the fingers on the skeleton that hung in their Science class. It wasn't until they were back at the table that rich noticed that other than the employees, there wasn't a woman in the entire establishment. "You guys better dig in" Adam said from his place at the head of the table.

"I'm not planning on throwing any of these good eats away come show time" he said as he was shoving one of the massive ribs into his mouth. "Showtime?" Rich repeated inquisitively as he listened to his stomach growl. He was still anticipating whether or not he was going to be able to partake in the platters of pleasantries now placed before them all. "Yeah, the girls put on a presentation after dinner is served, to get the guys in the mood," Sye said with a blush. "Mood for what?" Rich asked. "You'll see Sye said, you'll see."

It wasn't long before the already dim lights of the bar got even dimmer and the cat calls instantly began. Lights flickered from an ancient mirrored disco ball that Richard had never recalled seeing before, had now come down from somewhere in the ceiling. The room was suddenly filled with raunchy music. The men were jeering and Rich sat staring at the employee entry door intently, curious to see what all of the rage was about. The men suddenly broke into rowdy cheers. Rich followed their eyes now to see, not one but several, naked, luminescent females slowly slithering down the walls from the ceiling near the entrance. Rich's first thought was to whip out his cell phone and get a video of it to post on YouTube. But no sooner had he tried to turn it on, he realized that it was completely dead, not just without signal, but it wouldn't even power on. Rich thought this was very strange, since he always left his phone plugged into a charger, whether in his work vehicle or at home. Therefore he always had a full charge. Rich considered taking the battery out and putting it back in, but the scene playing out before him was like nothing he'd ever seen. Men lined up now around the makeshift dance floor. Seven luminescent females, all of which Rich immediately recognized from their previous visit, gyrated seductively in front of them all. Gio was first in line, hips now gyrating wildly in one direction; his long hair now flew in the other. The seven females all circled tightly around Gio until only his head and hair could be seen swaying almost violently above them. Then they all circled him. Each of them caressing him all over, taking their turn kneeling in front of him momentarily until he literally collapses to the floor between them. The circle of females finally unravels, leaving Gio laughing hysterically on the floor now behind them. The seven spread out in search of another volunteer. There was definitely no problem at all finding a participant. Judging by the men's many scoffing; they were now literally in a sexual frenzy. One by one they all took turns being the center of attention. Those waiting to go next were more than happy to remove those that had gone last from the middle of what had now literally became an arena.

The spectacle carried on, until all but one had volunteered himself to take part in the fiasco. Now all eyes were on Rich, as the women gestured for him to join them in the middle of the floor. Rich hesitated politely, but was quickly pushed into position by a barrage of men who had now already served their purpose in the dance. Rich was more than a bit nervous as the females now swirl around him, caressing his hair, his face, his arms, as their bodies moved in yet closer. Hands start to undress his lower extremities and Rich suddenly feels first cold hands then warm split lips on his manhood. Even though his head screamed for him to resist, Rich sensed himself giving in and letting go. Pulses and impulses wreaked havoc in both heads, as he felt one mouth and then another devours his now throbbing member.

Rich could feel himself about to either lose consciousness or pass out or both as he neared what he knew was about to be a mind shattering climax. It was at that exact second of release that Rich felt first an extremely sharp and stinging pain in his testicles and lower shaft. It was momentarily, followed by a painless euphoria, causing him to break into uncontrollable laughter right there on the middle of the floor. But Rich seemed to be the only one still laughing at this point. In fact, even the music had stopped now, as the shorter luminescent with the split lip now leans in close to Rich and sniffs the air around him. Then she let out a deafening shriek that made Rich pass out completely.

When he had awakened he found himself in what only felt to him like a damp, musky hole or cave. Rich couldn't see his hands before his face in the blackness. But he didn't need to see, to know that he was now totally naked in the murkiness of the chamber that smelled similar to fear and fresh meat. Rich felt around in the darkness, for anything that might have been there, a stick, a rock, his clothing, something. But all he felt was what seemed like warm mud between his fingers. Holding his digits up to his face, Rich could tell that the muck had a strong smell of iron to it, similar to rust. He stayed where he was, on his back. He spread his right hand out in front of him and then his left, to try to get some vision of the size of the area where he now lay. Rich rested quietly for a second, listening for any sound that might have given him a sense of his surroundings. The only sounds that he could hear seemed to be coming from inside his own body. Richard had no idea where he was, what time it was or how long he had been where ever it was that he was now. What he did recognize were two things, one that he had not had anything to eat but a donut with a cup of coffee since Friday morning and secondly, the noise emerging from his stomach was merely a reminder of the same.

Rich pulled himself up to a sitting position. He realized immediately that his stomach might not be aware of his current predicament. His manhood at this time knew that he was merely waking up and that was a good enough cause for it to demand to have to take a leak. Not wanting to just pee where he had been lying, Rich stood up, took two steps backward and felt that cold, moisture, feeling on his back once again. The temperature change didn't matter so much as the fact that he wanted to piss like a race horse and he needed to do it now. Standing naked against the wet wall, he closed his eyes and let go, peeing as if he had been holding it for not simply hours but days.

It was not until Rich had reopened his eyes that he had been met with shock and almost total amazement. His urine was now for whatever reason bioluminescent and now casting an eerie green glow across the floor in front of him.

Rich couldn't believe his eyes as they followed the luminescent stream along a groove in the mud. They then settled against what looked in the faint glow, like a large stone or boulder only feet away from where he now existed. Rich walked slowly over to the object, allowing his eyes to adjust as best they could to the subdued green radiance as he got closer. He reached his right hand forward to grab hold of the object. He thought if nothing more, he might be able to use it as a table, or even as a seat. But the contact allowed him to acknowledge right away that the object wasn't solid like a rock. Instead it was soft and covered in some kind of a cloth like material. At that exact moment, the strong odor of his own warm urine quickly gave way once again to the potent smell of raw meat.

Observing that there was nothing on the other side of the thing, Rich walked around the lump and looked again. Whatever the material was, it is dark and almost impossible to make out in the now almost none existent glow of his now fading stream.

Rich was less concerned about the fact that his urine was now luminescent than he was with the fact that he maybe wouldn't have to pee again for hours. Although he knew he would probably be sitting here in the dark for hours waiting to go again. The scent of raw meat was becoming almost over powering as he bent over and scooped up some of his own pee from the mud in the corner. He cupped it cautiously in his hands and knelt down on one knee in front of the almost two feet in diameter clump before him on the cave floor. Rich leaned in close, carefully cupping the bioluminescent urine in his hand and bringing it right down to the level of the bundle seated still on the floor in front of him. It was at this time that his breath caught in his throat, making it impossible to breathe for almost half a minute. The lump before him was not made of cloth but covered in clothes. The material was a thick brown textile, much like the material of his uniform. He took his free hand and allowed one finger to gently press against the material. He knew almost immediately what the sticky substance now on the tip of his two fingers now felt like.

Rich allowed the remainder of the glow in the dark pee to now flow from his palm. It spilled lightly down the front of the bundle of brown material, laminating the fabric on contact and a sewn on name tag that Rich could now clearly see. Even though black stains covered two of the letters, he could still make out the name Carl.

It was at this point he could hear movement in the murkiness close to him. Figuring that it wouldn't make much sense to turn around, he stared into the blackness. He sat not moving and listened and tried to imagine exactly where whatever was now in the room with him. He was sure that he heard something in the darkness behind him. So he knelt, still, listening for the faintest wisp of material rubbing. But all he sensed was his heart beating wildly in his chest.

Just then Rich had really begun to believe again that he was there alone, and that there had been nothing to fear but his fears, the brightness took on another pale glow. This time a dark Mediterranean blue cloaked the room in dim light. Rich sat silently, not even breathing, fearing any second was about to be his last. Focusing on the lump in front of him while his eyes adjusted to the soft gleam had helped him to see a little better. But Rich wasn't precisely sure he truly wanted to find out what was about to be his final moment of his life.

At that instant Rich felt a palm gently grab his right shoulder and if the grip been a little tighter, he might have fainted in fear. The gentle touch had caused Rich to turn quickly, while still on one knee, to once again come face to face with the shortest of the six female underlings. It was not just her eyes but her bodily fluids were running just under her translucent skin, which had now set the room aglow.

Rich rose slowly before her, his own eyes never leaving hers. He soon came to tower over her, paying no attention to the fact that he presently stood before her, both totally nude and unarmed. He searched her eyes at once for some form of reasoning but found none. Rich extended his right hand out toward her as a gesture of peace, but she moved swiftly away from it, her luminescence showing even brighter as her pulse apparently quickened. She looked at his palm cautiously yet inquisitively before moving in closer, close enough actually that he could smell what his mind curiously categorized as dark liquid funk. She reached out a frail glowing arm and now Rich unconsciously leans back in fear. "What am I doing in here?" Rich questioned softly. "And where are my clothes and why am I naked in this, what is this place?" he asked getting louder with each question. The shorter underling with the cleft lip pressed one of her cold, thin fingers against his lips, silencing him instantly, her eyes still not breaking away from his own.

He suddenly found himself not only feeling safe, but instantly turned on, sensing his manhood start to grow right there in the darkness between them. Almost as if she had someway sensed his excitement her head tilted. It caused the light from one of her eyes to presently cast a dark ominous glow across the shaft of his manhood. Her face immediately took on a grimace, almost as if she'd abruptly been struck by an acute inner pain. Reaching down with gaunt, sharp finger tips she grasped his testicles between her fingers. Her claw like nails now carelessly scraped his vasectomy scar. Pressing her talon sharply into the sack of his scrotum she looked at him pleadingly. Ignoring the throbbing, Rich now prepared to answer her question, one she hadn't asked verbally but one that he had felt somehow through her very touch.

"It's a vasectomy scar," Rich said softly. I didn't want to have a bunch of kids outside of marriage, so I got the procedure back when I was eighteen." She looked Rich over even closer now, raising his testicles to let the light from her eyes to momentarily set them aglow. Rich couldn't help but allow his eyes to drop down.

He once again was shocked to see the blood vessels all along the shaft of his penis as well as the smaller veins that made their way through the sack of his testes, glowing much the same as his urine had done earlier. The sack itself was black and without form. This fact seemed to cause her great sorrow. 'Listen, I've not eaten in like forever and I'm starving, you think maybe I could get something to eat?"

The shorter underling with the cleft lip reached down, ripped a large piece of meat and skin from the bundle of flesh. The fabric then dropped it into Rich's hand before going completely dark.

Rich had apparently passed out, because when he woke up lying on the ground, he found it easier to see his surroundings. The opaque light seemed to be coming from nowhere in particular, yet everywhere at the same time. He could also see clearly that the lump on the blood covered floor was the torso of his friend and coworker Carl, but it no longer looked terrifying to Rich. In fact the smell of it was actually causing his stomach to rumble even more. Walking around the small confined space, he could observe that the place where he had been laying wasn't caked with mud or smelled like iron, but instead with blood and dirt. Although he was glad to see the mound of flesh that she dropped into his hand now lay on the floor. The idea that he may have eaten it didn't so much gross him out as pissed him off that he might have really missed out on a meal.

As he leaned in to take a closer look, Rich couldn't help but notice the light over the cluster of meat got brighter as well. It was then that he, for the first time, looked down at his own nakedness. Rich expected to see his body concealed in the same slimy blood and dirt that covered the floor and walls.

Instead he was spotless, and he knew this because his own flesh now took on the hue of alabaster. The veins that were running through his thin tinted skin showed streaks of light as luminescent blood coursed through the body that was now his. He elevated his arm and the level of light in the room began to rise. Then he lifted another limb, the light in the room became bright again. Rich then looked up and saw that there appeared to be no ceiling in his cell. It was as if someone had stuck a large, round peg deeply into the ground, causing a deep trench, removed the stick, and then dropped him into the hole. His arms were still raised, as his eyes searched the heights for any sign of light, but saw none. What he did see was something ominous, about sixty feet above him and slithering quickly down the sides of the whole toward him. As it was sliding slime like down the wall, Rich scanned around the room for anything that he might be able to use as a weapon, but saw nothing. Then as the object slithered closer, it seemed to have turned on a light source, and was now using it to help Rich to recognize it. It was Shorty with the split lip and Rich suddenly felt a lot more at ease. He opened his mouth to ask her why he was here and for her assistance in getting back to where ever he had come from. But the sound that escaped his lips had scared even him. The strange thing was, as it became evident that she understood, she slid down to where he was and let him know that she had a plan.

After coming completely down to the floor she made a low rumbling sound that sounded like words, but with such deep baritone that Barry Whyte would have been proud. She stared back up into the darkness that she merely slithered out of, this time beckoning for him to follow her as she started back up the wall. He didn't understand how he could have, and stood briefly reaching up toward her, the way that a toddler would reach for an adult once it had gotten tired of toddling. Like a pissed off mother she then screams at him, her screech caused him to jump, totally out of dread. But his leap of fear had been more than even he had anticipated. Like a powerful sneeze it had launched him up against the wall behind where he had just been standing and he had stuck there, high on the wall, his back sticking to it like spit on a chalk board. Richard smiled briefly, his mouth contorting strangely as it too adjusted to the new him. Rich moved smoothly up the enclosure on his spine, his feet kicking angrily behind him as he rose faster and faster up the side of the dirt hole.

He probably would have advanced right on passed her had she not screamed that eerie scream once more, alerting that she had turned and was now in a horizontal tube. She once again allowed herself to fluoresce, but only momentarily, long enough for him to realize her location. Similar to a young hatchling following its parent, he followed her still deeper into the pipe.

As what now become the new Rich, scurried along in the skid marks of his Underling Mother. Now scampering to keep up, she stayed a few yards ahead of him. Rich shortly realized why she had remained in front of him as he trampled loudly through the tube. He had no way of knowing if they were alone in the tubes, or if other things were in the distance that could put a damper on an already weird day. He soon found out when the tube was suddenly filled with a shrill cry like nothing Rich has ever in life heard before.

He then turned to look back in hopes of seeing what caused the sound, when he came to realize the noise had somehow come from him, from where? He still didn't know. It might have been a fart for all he knew. What he understood for sure was that something had him and was pulling him backwards much faster than he had been going onward. The entire tube was now brightly illuminated, as the fear in him showed through. He couldn't feel anything holding him, but he also couldn't kick forward as he sped to the rear of the pipe. Rich managed to glance down just in time to observe what appeared to be like a massive fleshy muscular organ wrapped tightly around his lower extremities. On the far end of that forked tongue all Rich was able to see were rows of what resembled jagged teeth. Richard could not tell whether they were gyrating wildly or if the fact that he was spiraling toward them simply made them seem that way. Either way, he noticed that he was about to be something's dinner.

Fearing his impending demise, he closed his eyes tightly in anticipation of the brief pain that he knew would course through his body momentarily, as razor sharp teeth shredded limb after fluorescent limb. But the sensation didn't come. What came was a protective mother, not yet willing to lose her new pet. Had anyone seen the events that followed, they might have thought she had instantly morphed into what may have looked something resembling a giant.

She looked a like a flying illuminated bloodworm with one hell of a jet propulsion system. In less than a second, she had completely devoured Rich and most of the intruder's tongue. Almost as if to say, 'If I can't have it for a pet I'll eat it myself before I'll allow you to."

Now with her new possession safe within her confines, Split Lip set about the task at hand, making sure that the invader perceived that its intrusion had been greatly unappreciated. Once she made short work of that situation, she went completely black. She disappeared back down the tube in the direction that she had been headed before she had been forced to devour her new pet. Split Lip navigated her way through total darkness by sensory perception. Taking sharp curves and quick turns without ever touching the tube's slime splattered walls. In no time she came into an area where she finally felt at ease enough to allow her luminescence. No sooner had she allowed her arterial lights to shine, was she joined by many others of her kind.

They all swirled with each other violently, yet one never touched the other. They Twisted and twirled, like separate molecules of water, all caught up in the same body of sea, now coming together to make a wave. The convergence was for them a way of sharing information, and Split Lip now both relayed and received pertinent data for the monumental task now so close at hand. The underlings all glowed now in anticipation. They knew that in large groups they would have nothing to fear from even the most massive mammal in the upper realms. Their parent's and ancestors by and by foretold of the day when they would rise up against the Top Dwellers and rightfully claim what they felt they had every right to possess. The freedom to both protect and revel in the land where they and their forefathers were Born and had the privilege to enjoy. Today they would go to the surface and take back the earth from those that must destroy in order to build. The elders put a plan in action long ago and now all of the signs told them that it was presently their turn to make a difference. Each being its own individual now came jointly in huge numbers, to cause a wave of utter destruction on the regions above. Returning to the darkness was not an option, plans were in place and the time was now.

Winter had been extremely unforgiving; the east coast had been wiped out by massive snow and ice storms. Even Florida reported a record snowfall. Places like Wrens Georgia and North Augusta South Carolina lost electricity in the beginning of what many residents were heard to say after round one was, "the worst ice storm I've ever seen in all the born days of my life." Word soon spread by way of those who had generators and still had a cell phone signal, that the power could be out anywhere from an hour to a week. What they hadn't counted on was the massive floods that would completely wash out the eastern grids and nearly ninety percent of the eastern shoreline as well. Three days of temperatures above 70 in the Northern United States, and southern Canada, caused all four of the frozen great lakes, to all begin to melt for the first time in recorded history. The rapid thaw over flooded their banks.

Only days before, bridges that for years had connected major highways across the country, allowing commerce to flow freely had been washed away. Flood waters from the melt down, along with an unforeseen force in California within a matter of minutes has made landfall. The heavy rains quickly overtook Klamath Beach and then it swallowed up almost everything west of Nevada State.

As flood waters proceeded to rise expectedly in the Mid-West, people along the mighty Mississippi River continue to prepare for the major flooding they knew came each year after the hard winter freeze.

Spillways and aqueducts in and around the city of New Orleans rose higher each day. As waters from the far north, west, and northwest

Michigan began its trek south close to Cohasset Minnesota all the way down to where it finally branched out like fingers into the Gulf of Mexico.

Had anyone been standing beside the seawall, near the car port of the now deserted Rusty Anchor, they might have noticed the water gushing out from the big pipes beneath the parking lot into the aqueduct, where just weeks ago there had been but a trickle. But even the most alert pair of eyes would have missed the mass exodus of the Underlings from the grated pipelines. Like torrential rains, they poured out into the watercourse. Some of them set out north against the stream through the Inner Harbor Navigation Canal. They followed that route first into Lake Pontchartrain, then into The Rigolets, that would lead them past Rabbit Island and into The Gulf Of Mexico. Others had aimed toward the east from the interface, along the Intra-coastal Waterway, until they spilled out by the millions into Lake Borgne, then into Chandeleur Sound, at the mouth of the Gulf of Mexico. The millions more that stayed the course, were presently flowing quickly north in the strong south bound current of the Mississippi River headed due north. Their numbers were growing by the minute with each major city that they passed through.

At The Port of Baton Rough-Deep Water, they were joined by millions of other Underlings from that area. There was a slight color variation but they knew that they were all related. This scene continued to repeat itself north all along the massive winding river. An exact third of them headed to the starboard fork that became the Ohio River.

A north eastern route led them directly to Lake Erie and another branch of the Ohio River took millions more first into Pittsburg and then north into the Allegheny Mountain range to once again join those who continued north into Cincinnati in Lake Eerie. Others that persisted north along the Mississippi had become part of a mass of billions by the time they reached Minneapolis Minnesota. Underlings from all five of the great lakes, as well as the thousands of lakes in

Minnesota and Wisconsin now merged with them, in numbers ever before heard of and colors never seen, and on a mission.

After all the Great Lakes froze over, the snow continued to fall; leaving twelve to fifteen foot drifts atop the inlets in some places, ice caves in others . It all added up to bad news come melting time. Weather men had forecasted their expectations of the possibility of severe flooding around spring. But what came next had been totally unexpected would indeed have been a major understatement.

As soon as the power grids shut down, people fearing either starving or freezing to death, went into self-preservation mode. Supermarkets, whose expensive security systems were now basically useless, became first priority targets. Windows in Wal-Marts nationwide had been smashed out within minutes of the outage. Even in stores that were still open when the power failed. Men and women walked out with full carts of merchandise, some brave enough to come out with two carts. Other even braver souls had actually gone back to claim even more ill-gotten gain.

Youth's now filled shopping carts with electronic equipment that they couldn't have used even with a generator. Gas has now become a commodity worth dying or taking a life for. Every bridge and overpass that eventually leads anywhere has been damaged to the point of impassable, either by, sink holes, earthquakes, floods, or pot holes so big that you could no longer see bottoms in them. Abandoned and currently useless, high-end vehicles lined roads and parking lots, their usefulness greatly diminished as many become nothing more than hazardous burned out shells. Even in these turbulent and turmoilistic times, gunshots echoed, as mankind continue to slaughter their own for material possessions and to molest their own for temporary sexual gratification.

The uprising had begun on February 14th, Valentine's Day at 6:53 PM, a time which marked the first full snow moon of the New Year. Underlings all over the globe had long waited for this day and for the opportunity to make a difference. Their mission would change the lives of Underlings worldwide, living and not yet born, from this day forward. At sunrise on the 14th, a migration of underlings from all over the world, set out on a course to reach the deepest cold water sources on earth in massive numbers.

They kinetically raised the water temperature, using their sensory perception, enhanced by the huge amount of individuals sending out the same high pitched electro kinetic impulses at the same moment. The earth's water temperature rose globally to sixty eight degrees within a matter of hours. Sixty-eight degrees was the perfect temperature for all the earth's aquatic vegetation including eighty percent of ocean life. Everything from the ocean's vast assortment of single celled ameba, planktons and phytoplankton's all the way up to the oceans largest sea mammals.

By the time the sun was ready to set in the east, millions upon millions of the luminescent Underlings took their rightful place in the frozen deep. They began to prepare for an uprising like none ever attempted on earth.

At exactly 6:53 PM, a shrill siren cry could be heard piercing the cold late winter air all over Lake Superior. The low pitched, high scream like sound had started out so depleted that only very sensitive ears could have picked up the nearly subsonic squeal. As it intensifies, the noise rapidly reverberated through Lakes Michigan, Huron, Eerie and Ontario before the resonate could actually be heard by human hearing. By then nothing could have reversed the changes not taking place. As the temperature of the deep waters began to rise quickly, the ice began to melt. Snow drifts seem to virtually drown as they quickly fall down. Ice caves that had been carved by wet blowing snow instantly froze in place and Sank fast as water temperatures rose causing water levels to climb even faster. At this moment the Underlings opened up to sing a combined song of utter chaos and assured total destruction for all mankind.

Marquette, Munising, Newberry, Paradise, Rudyard and St. Ignace, Sugar Island Neebish Islet, St. Joseph Island, Drummond Island and

Cockburn Island, all which formed the land masses that separated Lake Superior from Lakes Huron and Michigan was quickly swallowed up, making three great lakes into one massive one. The entire land mass between the state of Wisconsin and Sault St Marie Canada was gone in a matter of minutes, leaving hundreds of thousands either dead or dying.

Overflow from Lake Huron quickly causes Georgian Bay to run over its banks by over fifty feet, pushing the rivers of Owen Sound and Nottawasaga Bay, deep into Wasaga Beach. The Nottawasaga river was literally obliterated and churned under as waters rush south across the mainland. Before very long the Nottawasaga Bay and Lake Simco in Ontario became one, leaving the city of Toronto an Island, but only temporarily.

Soon Toronto, Mississauga and Hamilton Ontario and all of its many residences businesses, corporations, factories and citizens were but historic artifacts deep beneath a new nation. All five of the great lakes had now become united. Over spillage had then caused Lake Michigan to overflow. The coast spilled from Menomonee Falls, just north of Milwaukee on the west levees, to Benton Harbor on the lower eastern shore. By 7PM a heavy fog blinded the fact that Lake Michigan's water level had not only risen by over forty-two feet since 6:53 PM, but it also tilted by 28 degrees to the south, the direction it was now headed. A 42 foot tall wall of water rose between Waukegan Illinois and South Haven Michigan. The surfaces 28 degree tilt gave it what might have looked like a backwards wave affect, as it rushed south at over eighty miles per hour.

At 6:54 PM Gillson Park was literally sheared off, by rushing waters. It washed over the jetties at the mouth of North Shore Channel with a big force. Some of the large boulders used to construct the base of the jetties and the manmade beach would wind up in the remnants of Soldier Field on Chicago's south side. The raging water instantly dredges out the mouth of the channel. The edge of the backwards wave literally dug Lincoln Park out of what had long been its pivotal location at Montrose Harbor. It instantaneously conjoined Montrose, Belmont and Lincoln Harbors as one. The massive destruction it caused there was within a matter of minutes roaring through what had now become the remnants of Olive Park and Navy Pier.

Chicago momentarily became first a peninsula and then an island, as the once calm channel grew to almost four miles in width before reaching the Chicago River and down town. It had become a peninsula in a matter of seconds, an isle for only a matter of minutes. By 7PM the tops of Chicago's highest sky scrapers were still above water. What now remained of their steel frames was now weirdly contorted, like some ancient sculpture from years past.

Violent rapids flowed through what not so long ago been the forty story windows along both North and South Lake Drives. By 7:15 pm everything from Aurora Illinois to South Bend Indiana was under more than seventy feet of water. By 7:41 Springfield Illinois, Indianapolis Indiana and Cincinnati Ohio had all suffered the same fate. Had the electrical grids not been destroyed by the winter ice storms 28.2 million people might very well have been electrocuted as they drowned in the massive floods. 8:08 pm, Springfield Missouri, Nashville Tennessee and Winston-Salem North Carolina were all flooded so completely that entire mountain ranges were now flattened.

At sunset, an earthquake with a preliminary 4.4 magnitude hit South Carolina, Epicenter near Edgefield S.C., signaling the end of the first full day above ground for the recent residents. Just as quickly as waters had risen, they receded, leaving in its wake a massive, muddy mess, entangled in debris and corpses. The underlings would have no problem finding foods for the feast tonight. Young Underlings detached heads, posting them on the ends of branches like trophies, little ones carried arms and legs for elders. They gathered beside the east coast, an area recently known as the Appalachian Trail, was now ocean front. As bodies and body parts were assembled, they were pulled into and then separated by pieces before being washed clean in the waves along New Beach.

With the apparently male ones, it was soon found that most of them had three large appendages dangling beneath them. If you were to grab the three and pull, it basically dislodged all of their innards, leaving only their tasty heart intact. With the females you simply slid a talon down the center of their bellies and pulled. Everything usually came out in one swift tug. The thicker ones were skewered with big broken branches and heated over huge steel vats that the Underlings had salvaged from the bottoms of the barges they collected in Manhattan on New Year's Day. Once they were thoroughly heated on one side they were rolled onto the other side and heated a while longer. If this were done properly their bodies will secrete oils that could then be used for many things, such as waterproofing their weapons and even for cooking up the thinner more stringy ones. Once the steel tanks had become a little over half full with oil, arms, legs, feet and fingers were thrown into the hot oils and allowed to sink to the bottom of the steel barrel.

Once a limb had reached its proper consistency for consumption it would float to the top of the oil, where it then be scooped up and quickly devoured. The heads on the sticks were also coated with this same oil, but only after the oils had cooled.

The Underlings found that if they soaked the heads with the oils, that the stringy hairs on them would soak it up and each one could serve as a burning torch, capable of providing light in even the darkest places for long periods of time. Nothing gets wasted; even innards that had been so unceremoniously ripped out of the bodies would serve either as fish food or fertilizer. Bones left over after the feast would be collected. They were then cleaned and fashioned into ceremonial garb to be worn by Namow every year at this time, to symbolize the concurring of the surface dwellers. Survivors were enslaved in dark tombs below ground, and were well treated, for a people who had been destroying their own habitat for years and obviously had no concept of life without leadership.

The Underlings had found out shortly after capturing their first humans, that it took very little to sustain them. Each time one died, it was quickly deboned and its meat ground, pressed, heated and served to the remaining beings. Feeding them calmed them, made them lethargic thus easily manageable. Once they had over eaten they went into a nightly hibernation. It was during these nocturnal hibernations that they became totally docile. The Underlings also found that if you picked fruit and allowed it to rot in large quantities; they could use the extracted liquid as an aphrodisiac. It caused their male human slaves to become aroused yet submissive, which in turn made it easy for collectors to retrieve the much needed spermatids that they required for good strong reproduction to take place.

The Underlings experimented with reverse semination, implanting their own embryos into female surface dwellers. The babies had grown too rapidly and were also found to be more susceptible to human ailments. The infants needed constant hibernation and were physically dependent and had other various attachment issues. They were also susceptible to temperature change and to cancers. The Underlings knew that the only way to terminate their reign here on earth would be to end their lives. So any and all women surface dwellers were simply killed and fed to the male surface dwellers.

Namow had not been born of a royal bloodline; in fact she too had been part of an experimental project. In earlier, more primitive times, any stolen male ground dwellers were slaughtered soon after capture. Surface dweller females were often enslaved long term, as they had been found to be useful in many ways. They're instincts had endowed them with a gut fortitude that was not only rare, but would also prove to be lethal in the wrong possession. In those times, males were still deboned, their meat ground, pressed, heated and served to the remaining female humans. Even at feeding time, the female Surface dwellers remained guarded. They smelled their food before they ate it, then ate slowly, dissecting it as they continued. It was as if they were trying to figure out what had given it its gamey flavor. Also unlike the larger men, they seemed to have a strong sense of loyalty to their cause.

Unfortunately their cause had been altered by lack of knowledge and something they were heard crying about many times before dying, things called husbands and children. Though they had no concept of these strange characteristics, every Underling knew that survival meant being able to adapt, not only to adversity but environmental diversity as well.

Surface dwelling females ate only enough to sustain themselves. They too suffered a need to hibernate soon after the sunset, often for up to a third of the entire day. The females were so much more active after hibernating and actually seemed re-energized, as though they were somehow fueled by sleep. Their cries were shriller, but their endurance appeared to be ever flowing. These women were also a lot less docile during hibernation. They could lay in the darkness without stirring for long periods, but the slightest stir caused them to quickly manifest into the protector. They too had something that not only their males lacked but that the Underlings needed as well. They could get the males of their species to do just about anything for them, simply by looking at them or stroking them in a certain way. This baffled the Underlings more than anything else about those who lived on, literally left their mark everywhere that they went. This power of persuasion was what first prompted the Underlings to consider the possibilities of what they might possibly gain by a mixing of species genetically.

It was after noticing this rare and wonderful attribute did Underlings begin to use the Surface dwellers not just as slaves but as scientific experiments as well. Many females were bled and dissected; they were often stripped of their smooth, textured skin, which Underlings chewed like chewing gum to tighten the jaw muscles. DNA was still being harshly extracted from male Underlings and implanted in Surface dwelling females in hopes of somehow conjoining the two species, but there were flaws, Cancers that lessened the overall appeal of the total process. Those that lived longer were too dependent on long hours of sleep. The larger ones were gangly and clumsy and their offspring slow to grow, requiring years of cultivating and guidance before they proved to be better off boiled.

Many years of experimentations and failures passed, before finally, a right combination had come together totally by accident. One of the impregnated females died and her body had been deboned and ground after her viscera and smooth skin were removed. One of the male underlings snatched up the innards and enjoyed them as a snack. For his dishonesty, he ended up with a massive growth in his insides that continued to grow to almost three times the size of his head within three seasons. Not being accustomed to pain the male Underling persisted as usual until one day he strained while pooping and the bothersome mass popped out. He might simply have buried it as they always do when taking a poo, had it not been wiggling and crying in the hole beneath him.

The male quickly retrieved the thing, still encased in its sack and stared at it with every intention of eating it, until it looked into her eyes. From that moment on he would have to do whatever she required and soon so did all of the others, not because she asked but because she persuaded.

Her powers of persuasion quickly endeared all who gazed upon her. Her wisdom was sought after by the old as well as the young. Her notoriety established a force. Her fierceness demanded loyalty and her gift of domination made her queen amongst her kind. Namow soon became aware of her abilities as well, using every opportunity to persuade those around her to do her bidding. What Namow needed of them wasn't physical things, what she asked of them, commanded of them in fact was respect. In return she would share with them stories that manifested in her dreams, something else that the Underlings did not have the power to do. Before Namow they had been like schools of fish, swimming aimlessly between the bubbles. There was no hope for change, no seeds of yearning and no desire for more.

As others came and went over the vast years, Namow held constant. Unlike any Underling before her or since, her genetic makeup had allowed her to live well into her fourth century. Yet she shined as brilliantly as their youngest and could fight with as much strength as the most aggressive young male Underling.

Namow told stories of how her parents once lived on the top and of how they'd been temporarily enslaved by the surface dwellers after being caught up in huge nets in the vast waters that covered the earth. She told of how they had been pulled from the seas and on massive vessels where they were deposited among thousands of dead and dying fish onto the deck. Namow informed them that this was the very first moment they had ever come into close contact with the pallid habitants from the land. They adapted to spending most of their time at sea, swimming with whales and dolphin, hunting with the orca and following the ocean currents to where ever it might lead to. Her mother and father had been slaughtered while she was still inside of her father's belly, brutally bludgeoned and then thrown back into the deep. She told them of how she had been beaten right out of her fathers's body and kept on display in an invisible cylinder for other pale people to stare at. Some were banging on the unseeable walls with open palms, causing electrical Impulses that strengthened her though distorting her sense of direction as well as her perception of being.

Namow then told of how after many untold moons she was forced to eat a substandard diet of only sardines and live in stagnant water, which now reeked of her own bodily waist and excrement. That night, she cried out to the full moon, for death to arrive and take her away from this meaningless existence. A cry that appeared not to go unheeded, as it had caused her invisible enclosure to momentarily become visible.

The enclosure became billions of tiny cracks, only seconds before exploding outward, sending both Namow and the putrid smelling water crashing and splashing onto the floor. Namow wasted no time heading in the same direction she had seen the last pale person go, until she once again came upon yet another invisible road block. From this place she can observe the river's edge and strange lights and structures that soared into the sky. Spiraled smoke killed the trees and caused both the water and the air they all breathed to become foul and tainted. Having stored up for so long, electrical impulses given to her by the constant banging on the invisible enclosure, Namow now concentrates on the vision on the other side momentarily. She told herself that the barrier she couldn't see was not really there, lunging forward and through it. She slithered on her belly like a walking catfish, across vast expanses of flat, hard earth. Namow told them of how she had then vowed vengeance, not just for her parents, but for all who had ever been taken in the nets to never return.

Namow never mentioned that she dreamt all of this, for they knew not of dreams or imagination. What they do know was that she is wiser and stronger and that she was to be respected. She did not tell them that she had been born of a lowly cleaner, who had eaten her father's discarded innards, thus devouring his embryo and later becoming her mother. Namow thought the story far too complicated, besides, she greatly appreciated the attention.

The large number of human slaves held in captivity by Namow became an issue. She had the ability to house them, not so much comfortably but safely, so as to get the most work out of them. she had each of them summoned before her, so that she could stare into their faces, their eyes and their desires. She wanted to see what it was they had that yielded them comfort. Namow used her power of persuasion to search deep into the eyes of thousands, maybe even hundreds of thousands of men. She realize all the things that brought them solace, were items they could hoard and use braggingly to make themselves look superior to their fellow beings. She had personally sought out to acquire semen from the one that named himself Rich. She allowed him a glimpse at a florescent tattoo of what he had called a Walther PPK, which had suddenly appeared on her upper thigh.

Namow had no idea what it was, but it was what she saw when she looked into the deepest parts of him through his eyes. Rich was excited by tattoos and guns. So Namow fabricated a tattoo of his favorite weapon and allowed his brain to tell him it was now actually visible on her upper thigh. It was the first place he looked as they approached the group of males in the bar near the wall. Inside they quickly realized that the men had created amongst themselves an ambience of perversion. It was this same perverted atmosphere that she'd recreated in the minds of the slaves she still housed. In their thoughts, whenever they saw each other, they'd perceive a situation that harbored their own perversions.

Some fancied biker bars, some in strip clubs, others nightclubs, but they all seemed very comfortable in The Anchor Bar. So every evening after their duties, chores and anal probes and other explorations, they are all put together in a large pit. There once again they would become joyous, drinking themselves into an alcohol induced sexual frenzy. It was at this moment that she would use her morphing ability to show each of them their idea of the ideal mate. Namow did this by appearing to be the woman each of them wanted to see. Her abilities to morph allowed her to turn into a larger shape, a smaller figure, or even a few different formations at once. This is why surface dwellers had seen several women when this entire time there had been only one.

Namow had found that her technique worked well in most cases where she may otherwise have looked vulnerable. If she had appeared alone its very likely she might have become a target of a well-known Surface dweller's aggression. She had seen long ago the torment that the male Surface Dwellers had done to their own kind. Instead of protecting the link that provided them life, they chose to scar, agonize and torture the only one capable of guaranteeing that their species continued. Namow watched from the high side of the pit, as the men drank and reveled to the memories of music presently playing in their heads. She took a mental count of the sixty or so and quickly realized which were missing. She then deducted those that had been eaten and came to the conclusion that the only one now unaccounted for was . . . she reached down and rubbed her stomach thoughtfully before heaving convulsively, as if in major discomfort, as she regurgitated her last meal. It was still completely whole; a little slick with neon mucus, but none the worse for wears.

She tossed rich unceremoniously against the panel before he had even caught his first gulp of air. She watched as his limp body trickled down the side of the dirt intact, which quickly became an interior wall at The Rusty Anchor. As Rich's frame reached the floor he slowly slid to his feet, used the back of his arm to wipe the slime off of his face and then walked out of the men's room. With the exception of Carl and Skip, the guys were all there, washing down beers and waiting on him. "Why does it take you so long to pee?" Adam asked even before he retraced his steps to their shared table. "Just lucky I guess," Sye said. "I figured for sure you'd stay in there until the girls all came back."

It was at exactly that moment that the room, once illuminated only by the slave's own fluorescents, now became bathed not in the opaque green, but a soft blue color. The change in lighting instantly summoned hoopla from the recipients in the bar. They were clear the light show was signaling one thing and one thing only, the arrival of the ladies. At the top of the cave, high above them, Namow pored herself onto the ground like water from a vase. As she spilled out along the edges of the large hole, Namow then allowed herself to re-solidify, but not as Namow. She appeared at the bottom of the cavity as all six of those sultry, sexy and sought after sisters. The six of them wiggled down the dirt wall, amongst cat calls and other things that men will say. Rich and the crew stood once again staring at the gyrating figures beneath an ancient disco ball.

The guys all took turns pushing their way toward the front to be serviced, but this time things were different in Rich's eyes. Rich now understood the real reason the women came out each night. In reality, the only purpose they were here was to milk them of their DNA. In fact Rich didn't know how he knew, but in an instant he realized that each of them were about as expendable as used Styrofoam cups. Rich remained in his seat, while the others literally went into a sexual frenzy, gyrating and rotating wildly across the floor, each awaiting their chance to donate to the cause. Knowing what he somehow knew, Rich tried hard to disappear into the darkness and go unnoticed and he basically did.

Once the offerings had been given and the collections taken, each man simultaneously leaves the room. All would awaken hours later, refreshed, and enveloped in memories of deed that never took place. Rich couldn't help but wonder, what would eventually become of them, or of mankind for that matter. He didn't even ask this time to participate in the gathering. He made his way back to his solitary den, just him and that big lump on the floor of what had at one time been Carl. Allowing his own inner light now to shine, Rich made a detailed blueprint of his surroundings. He did not know why, but he felt it important to do so, so he did.

Once he had totally mapped out the small space, Rich settled into an area where he allowed his subtle glow to dim considerably. He then crouched in a corner and prepared for slumber. Something else Rich had noticed was his inability to nap for any amount of time as of late. Although there was nothing in the hole to make noise, Rich continued to hear noises in his subconscious, each time he would try and close his eyes in a futile attempt at sleep.

These noises were nothing he had ever heard. Still they felt standard to him, almost as if it were a language that he had once known. Little did he know, it was a lingo that he was now only just beginning to learn. As he sat in his corner, now praying for sleep sounds and pictures in Rich's head continued to flicker like lights with a bad circuit connection. There were voices he could not yet understand but soon would. Images that he had never seen or heard before, will in the near future become as familiar to him as speaking, eating and napping were to him now.

Rich wasn't sure how long he had been sleeping or just in a state of limbo. When he opened his eyes, the first thing he noticed was the clump that had been Carl had been moved. Not only had the lump been shifted, but on closer inspection Rich realized that the bulge was now greatly smaller than it had been when he'd last seen it, shortly before he had fallen asleep or he'd blacked out. Rich leaned in close now, allowing his inner lights to illuminate the carcass. There was considerably less of Carl at this point. There were massive fresh tears in what was left of him. It looked as if something had taken a few huge chunks out of him, right here in this hole, while Rich had either slept or he had been rendered unconscious by whatever has been sharing the space with him.

He probably would have pondered this for quite a while longer, but the next noise Rich heard was definitely close and certainly not in his head. Above him he could now clearly see Namow traversing the walls of the hole, getting closer each second. He had no idea what was in store for him now, but if he was going to be a part it, then Rich felt that he had the right to know. Almost as if it were taking place in slow motion or in a strobe, Rich watched her draw near. He wanted to ask her why he was spared. He actually opened his mouth to state his opinion, but the sound that escaped from him wasn't the voice that he'd known to be his own. Neither had it spilled out from the area that his words had come from since the doctor had first smacked his ass in the delivery room. The loud squeal literally scared him, causing Rich to momentarily cower before her. What happened next startled him even more. She reached out, seizing a firm grip of Rich's testicles and dug one talon like nail deep into the empty sack of his scrotum.

For the average male this might have proven to be excruciatingly painful, but Rich had a vasectomy when he'd joined the military many years ago, to avoid finding out someday by accident that he was broke because of a lot of little Rich's. As she pressed the sharp, single digit into the void testicles, Rich's body is suddenly hammered with what feels to him like electrical impulses.

These impulses were then followed by pressure and then pain, like back in school, when Rich had been hit square in the nuts by a baseball slap shot to third base. Namow now released him, allowing him to drop on his knees in agonizing pain. The pain was so intense that he had remained in that position for only a matter of seconds before dropping completely to the floor and rolling partially into a fetal position. It was while he was in this totally vulnerable position that Namow had chosen to share with him and offer him an answer to his question.

"Your kind was placed in Paradise, one of each of your kind, to enjoy life, as all animals had done in this paradise, until you were placed amongst them here. Since the arrival of your kind here in paradise, you have caused total distinction of 19,621 other species, most of which you didn't even know existed and that had just as much right to be here as your kind. Your kind kills not just for food but for fun. From the very smallest insect to the largest living thing, you kill without discretion, remorse or reason. Your kind kills for trophy and for what you call sport. From the seas you take every kind of species without thought or malice to how and what way it might be replenished. You even pillage the land around you, killing trees that have adorned your Eden since before your ancestors, and for what, so you could build temporary shelter to house those that you call family and impress those that you call friends.

Not once do you consider how many years of life have now been taken for just your single dwelling alone. Thousands of years of forest, some thousands of years old, are being decimated each year, to provide comfort to a creature with less than a century in life span. Inside of that single century of life your kind has managed to destroy not just your Eden, but your own kind and yourselves as well. You take pleasure in things that cause you harm and in harming others. Your kind even save memories of the wrongs that you do, by having your victim either beheaded or solidified or both, to hang in your domicile as memory to your ability to master all that surround you. You fail to see that all of the things that you have horded are now dead things. You have taken all of the beauty that is all around you in your Eden and you have now killed it all and replaced it with solidified memories. Your kind destroys everything, yet you seem to appreciate nothing.

My kind has returned now, to clean up the mess, as we have done every 2000 years.

Namow continued her quiet rant, not verbally, but in Rich's mind and he clearly understood every word. Your kind has no concept of your reason for being here, yet you kill everything around you in an attempt to claim the right to call yourselves top species, yet you have not the strength in you to fight them face to face and without a weapon. Instead you set traps and kill from a distance, thus never allowing them the opportunity to fight or the chance to defend their own lives. It seems your kind is only interested in taking lives, not in preserving it.

The things that you value most are mostly things that have no value. Your kind was given a most precious gift, but all living things were given that gift, not just your kind. You have no right to deprive another living being, of your species or any other, life. You take what you can't give, even from those that could give so much more than you.

You see not the errors of your own ways. You have been given several precious commodities, each of which you have abused horribly for years. The first was life, yet your kind has done nothing to enhance your own that did not involve the taking of another's. The second is a sense of purpose. Your kind has no sense of purpose thus no reason to exist. And last but most important, time. Your kind already sleeps a third of your life away and you spend most of the time that's left of each day uselessly. Your kind believes that the only way to build something is to destroy other things. Your only goal in life is to make yourself seem somehow better than those like you. So now you are no longer a species to be feared. You are now instead, more like the animals that you've long herded and slaughtered for your food and for your comfort. So now, your kind will also be herded, you will be fenced in and lead to food and to drink, your meat will become a staple, bones as weapons and your skin as material for as you call it, luxurious living. Human kind's time has now ended, however, I have an offer for you that I am hoping that you are wise enough to consider, wisely, for if you don't, you will die, pretty much as the others have or will.

I can in no way offer you a life like the one you've had up until you learned of us, but the life I can offer you will far surpass the short existence you will have should you choose to decline my offer.

Although totally aware of what she was telling him and not being able to disagree with her on her claim, Rich still couldn't quite wrap his thoughts around what Namow was now offering him, but he was pretty sure that either way he looked at it, life as he knew it had now changed for good.

Rich's only question now was how good could it possibly be when his urine glows green his skin is already nearly translucent and he had just witnessed the destruction of over a third of the nation in his new pod of so called family. Rich looked at Namow concernedly now, wanting so badly to voice his own disagreement, but all he had been able to do was glow brighter and fart occasionally. "I've never even owned a BB gun, none the less a real gun", Rich thought in his head, "I'm no killer, hell I climb on a chair if I see a spider, and ok so I've been known to have a drink or two on Friday night after a hectic work week, but who hasn't done that?" As soon as the thought had exited his mind, Rich realized he could have worded it a little differently. "Now we must prepare for the next phase of our assault on the surface dwellers, which will take place on the next full moon, the Worm Moon. You will have until that time to make your decision. Until the rising of the Worm Moon, we shall celebrate our uprising.

A bit premature you might be thinking, for us to be celebrating so soon, but your kind has offered very little if any opposition, so this should be, in the words of your own kind, a cake walk." This being said, Namow reached out thin fingers in his directions, and waited for him to reach out to her in response, without either of them voicing or uttering a sound. "Come, for tonight we begin preparing for the celebration, we shall celebrate you and me becoming the next Adam and Eve.

Rich had seen the damage that Namow and the underlings were capable of after she had devoured him. Even though he hadn't eaten in what now seemed like days to Rich, he felt unusually full, as he watched the underlings swarm and swirl from one place to another. It was at this point that Namow beckoned for him once again. "You look to be in need of excitement", Namow said to him, reaching one glowing digit in his direction. Richard wasn't sure what she had in mind but he thought that anything would be better than sitting here watching little ones and the elders nibble on fingers by the light of the silvery moon.

Rich took the shimmering digit in his grasp and the two of them are instantly wisped to the beach front. Again without speaking she communicated with Rich, seemingly through some sort of mental telepathy. As the two of them entered the surf together, their eyes locked in a telepathic tease that had made his manhood rise at first with the waves rushing in and then from the blood now rushing furiously out.

Though the ocean had just been calm on New Beach, waves now rose and splashed violently around the two of them, though it seemingly not touching either. Rich allowed his focus to shift from Namow's eyes to her entire face, for the first time allowing himself to see the most beautiful woman he had ever seen. Their bodies stood stern against the waves. Rich's manhood stood stern against her belly as she begins to rise up with the tide, only to come down like a mouth on Rich's now massively swollen man member. Even staring into her face, Rich couldn't help but feel that it was some kind of hallucination, for what he was now feeling on his shaft was definitely a mouth, with a tongue that swirled its way along the veiny shaft before a full set of lips had totally sucked him in. In one thrust, Rich thought he could even feel the tonsils tapping against the head of his now sex starved man head.

Feeling more youthful then he had in years, Rich pounded with purpose, as though trying to make her have feelings that her kind knew not of, until he reached that point of jet propelled insemination, until what he was all but positive was a second mouth, sank its teeth into his testicles. Rich screamed out in an eerie cry, a sound all but drowned out by the waves, which now seem to be clapping and applauding their union. Namow was not to be denied a pleasure of her own.

As their abdomens pressed together tightly, a spiraling talon like object from her middle injected itself deep into his navel before burrowing south in his own birth canal and then back out quicker than Rich could have screamed ouch, had he even felt the pain. Within moments of the finally, Namow dipped into the surf and was gone. Rich was left standing alone in the now once again flat calm of New Beach. Rich made his way back to the beach alone and was quickly greeted by both babes and elders, who approached him as though he were a long and dear friend who had been lost at sea and had just now been washed up on the beach by a rogue wave. They surrounded him now, each of the elders now touching him gently, the babes gather all around him, taking turns touching his belly. They all stare at him in awe as he makes his way back up from the beach. Rich suddenly felt a little week and just as suddenly assumed that he might possibly had pulled a muscle or something out in the surf. Rich's stomach first seemed to be in knots, much like it had been that time when he'd entered a Texas chilly cook off.

By the time Rich had made it back to where he had originally been sitting on the beach, his stomach severely extended and bouncing around as if he had just consumed Mentos, Pop Rocks and Pepsi.
The continuous tumbling in Rich's stomach wasn't at all painful, what was painful was that now when he looked down he could plainly see what was either a hand or a foot pass across the inner walls of his luminescent and bulging belly.

Namow had not lied to him that he would be able to father a child again, what Namow hadn't told him was that during the pregnancy he would serve as mother as well.

By the time the Full Worm Moon Celebration had run until dawn, the giant vat of hot oil had gone cold and its tasty remnants long since devoured and digested, Rich was already in active labor. The elders all but carried him over to a large hole filled with water and Rich new for a fact that the intentions of the elder's had been to kill him when they'd tossed him haphazardly, yet directly into the center of a crystal clear pool. He couldn't help but wonder as he gulped to breath, why Namow would have ordered him executed while he was carrying their infant. It was not until he had resigned himself to the fact that he was about to die that Rich finally gave in and stopped holding his breath. His Lungs lunged, sucking in deeply, filling instantly with water. Rick's limp body floated lifeless to the bottom where it came to rest on a familiar lump. It was the thump that had jarred Rich back to full consciousness. He woke up in his usual hole, with its usual surroundings, but definitely not under what Rich would have called, "normal circumstances. His will to figure out when he had gone to sleep and who had brought him back here, wasn't nearly as important as how he was now going to give birth to an infant. Rich's body convulsed violently and he instantly rolled into a fetal position, grabbing his abdomen with both hands, as if he either had appendicitis or a very bad case of gas.

Deciding that he might get a little relief if he were to pass gas, Rich did what he'd normally do to cut a fart. Other than sounding a little wetter than usual, Rich thought, the sound still had the basic characteristics of a fart. Except his fart had now released into the hole, what had 1st looked to Rich, like long strings of thousands of tadpole eggs. The egg casings seem to be floating, Rich watched almost in amazement as the tiny tadpole like critters began to use saw like teeth to eat their way out of their casings. He then watched in horror as his own convulsions caused his stomach to split from his belly almost to his balls, and what he could only have described at that moment as his own appeared before his eyes for the first time.

Almost totally covered in an embryonic sack and other bodily fluids, the infant was hard to look at, but Rich still tried to imagine what it was going to look like once it's all cleaned up. It wasn't until then that Rich had noticed that the tiny tadpoles had now converged on the lump on the floor and had now gnawed it down to next to nothing.

The faster they ate the more they seemed to consume and the more they consumed the faster they seemed to grow, until they were each almost the size of ping pong balls. A few stragglers seeking scraps on the outer edges, seemed to be circling closer and closer to Rich and his new infant, as though they were closing in for the kill. The thought of this had brought Rich to full glow, as the first few mini mouths moved closer, one taking a chunk out of the edge of the sack and the baby's umbilical cord.

Rich sprang into action just as the second creature tore across his new infant's face, but the results it got were surely not the one it or Rich had expected. The infant had ripped into it fiercely, shattering it into tiny fragments, even before Rich had bolted toward the surface with it. With a desperate lunge, Rich pushed the infant out of the top of the hole and onto the same surface from which he had not so long ago been so unceremoniously thrown.

With the now thousands of tiny tennis balls with teeth tearing through the tube, trying to shred him and his new baby, Rich went into protection mode. But before he could do whatever it had been that he was going to do he felt himself being hurled out of the water by Namow. She had not deserted him, but had simply left him to do what it was that he had needed to do. In her arms she held the baby that the two of them had conceived together. It had long dark brown hair, beautiful blue-green eyes and a jagged rip in her upper lip where it had taken several savage bites out of whatever that thing was that had tried to make a meal out of the two of them. Rich looked down at his belly that had now already completely healed and then at the two of them before saying, "She has your smile."

Laila was a very special child in many ways. Conceived during winter storm Titan, she was first born, first born on a full worm moon, Namow's first and Rich's first.

Rich thought she was the most beautiful baby he had ever seen, for the first hour or so, as she had slowly progressed from infant to toddler to teen literally by day break. Rich suddenly finds himself more than two days without sleep and the father of a beautiful teen daughter whose eyes have already caught the eyes of every male underling for miles. They'd already gathered for the Worm Moon celebration, the birth of the new world's princess was just a thrown in extra added bonus.

For indeed Laila had been the very first Quarter Human to be born on the surface, after all, Rich was now only ¼ human. The split lip she'd had since birth not only gave her facial character, but it also made her and her mother look like identical twins. Even now they were the same size. Rich, somehow knowing that he had about half a day until the official start of Worm Moon, figured this would be a great time for him to catch some shut eye.

What Rich hadn't realized was that having a teenaged daughter was not about me time. Laila was anxious to go out and swarm with the others, but Rich was reluctant to let her out of his sight at such a young age. "Dad, play with me, she uttered to him in her own subterranean speak." "Well it's not like I was going to watch the Heat play the Lakers," Rich said jokingly. "Basketball is old- fashioned Dad, we're all within view of the new."

Rich tears to think that only yesterday he was almost middle aged and knew for certain that he would never know the joy of fatherhood, and now he had a beautiful teenaged daughter, calling him dad and vying for his attentions and his favor. "This is all just so sudden," Rich said as he ran his thin fingers through his even thinner hair. "Did you want we should play ball or something," Rich asked, not having a clue what to do with a girl like Laila; but as soon as they had gotten out into the crowd Rich realized that it was going to be a lot harder than he'd thought keeping up with a swarm of teenagers. Rich had somehow heard of their previous swarms, he wasn't quite sure how but he had. Just a few nights ago a bunch of them had morphed to the Orient where they had swarmed a train station, literally sawing their way through hundreds of people in a train station, injuring scores and killing tens in about an hour's time. Already having lost sight of them twice, Rich feared how he would explain to Namow how he'd lost their baby only a few hours after given birth to it. The swarm headed south along the shore of conception, as it would come to be known, and Rich soon realized that he had somehow memorized the scent pattern of every male in his daughter's swarm and that they were all now present and accounted for here along the shore; Laila however, was nowhere to be found. Rich was relieved that she wasn't with the youthful males, but at the same time deeply concerned that she was too young and possibly too vulnerable to be out here roaming and swarming alone, so soon in life.

Rich heard what sounded to him like the squeal of a badly wounded animal coming from just the other side of the nearest sand dune and instantly thought, "there are a lot of things that eat a lot of things around here that's for sure." As soon as Rich heard the sound the second time he knew for certain that Laila was in trouble.

Rich thrust himself almost immediately to the top of the mound, screaming for his daughter as he strolled forward. "Laila!" But Rich wasn't the only one anxious to scream Laila's name right at that moment. Rich found his little girl, wrapped in some weirdly passionate embrace with another Trans-subterranean. Rich wobbled back and forth atop the dune trying to catch his balance as his head swam and his vision and his mind refused to see what lay spread out before him on the lower border of the ridge. 'Dad, what in the world are you doing here?" Laila protested, not even attempting to hide the fact that her father had totally caught her with another female.

"Well I think you've got some explaining to do young lady," Rich said, trying to maintain some sort of fatherly composure. "Without so much as a wince, Laila simply said, Dad Amanda, Amanda my Dad."

MARCH 16TH FULL WORM MOON 1:08 PM

The weird silence that followed was only broken by the shrill scream signaling the start of a Full Worm Moon. The cry was immediately picked up by one and then all the Underlings, as they now vocalize side by side, the beginning of the ceremony.

As the voices became one, so had the bodies. The minions without delay merged like soap bubbles, or even better yet like beach foam, spreading near the water front for as far as the eye could see. As the shrill tone rose to what might have been ear shattering, the spume rushed east against the tide and against the sea's current. Within minutes the tribe formatted about a thousand miles off of New Beach. Others joined from hundreds and thousands of miles across the earth. They were in accord in both song and a seemingly demonic dance and it seemed to genetically align them with the universe itself. The clan got larger and so did the circle of dancers, currently swirling out over three thousand miles from the center. The spiraling band was now centered a long way out in the Sargasso Sea. But it's quickly thickening and constantly gyrating bands without delay spread out significantly west as Dakar and Senegal on the west coast of Africa, south east to Surinam and French Guiana off of the shores of Brazil. The expanse of bubbles amass at ocean and the dancing waves became yet more furious, spinning with the force of what would have been called, if there ever had been such a thing, a category-9 hurricane. Wind gusts along the outer belts alone already measured up to as much as 280 miles per hour. The self-made storm now possessed an eye wall that spread 500 nautical miles across and had already left Bermuda under close to a quarter mile of ocean.

The storm backed into Brazil, submerging, Suriname, Guyana, Venezuela, Columbia in South America and Panama City and all the isles of the Caribbean, even before lunging forward into Costa Rica, Nicaragua, Honduras, El Salvador, Guatemala, Belize, Grenada, Barbados, Dominica, Antigua and Barbuda, Saint Kitts and Nevis, Anguilla, Puerto Rico, as well as Haiti and the Dominican Republic before setting its sights on the Turks and Caicos and Exuma Islands off of the Bahamas. As the eastern fringe of the storm continued to batter what had been Bermuda, the western edge of the whirlwind completely battered Belize, Cancun and the entire Yucatan Peninsula at the mouth of the Gulf of Mexico. Not a thing stood between what was left of the

U.S. mainlan's south eastern shore, the Florida gold coast, but a matter of minutes.

The gale now tore a pathway from Corpus Christi to Key West, Mexico City to Miami. It totally devoured everything in its path, leaving nothing in its wake but a wave of utter devastation. By the time the eye of the storm had set its aim on Florida in its entirety. The huge storm, now more than twice the width of the Gulf of Mexico sent out massive spiraling bands which literally ripped out now long abandoned bridges that once linked the keys and boulevards of South Florida to the millions of tourist dollars that made it a key vacation destination for many years.

The storm makes a beeline straight up the center of the state, seemingly sucking energy from the warm waters of the Gulf of Mexico on the west and from the Atlantic Ocean on the east. The storm wasn't gaining its powers from the tepid waters of the Gulf or the Atlantic, but rather from the additional thick bodies joining in as the storm nears their zone.

The eye of the storm, like a giant looking glass into the heart of the devastation, now clearly shows what had for so many years been called the I-95 corridor, the transportation hub of the south east. The storm seemingly lined itself up west of I-95 and barreled straight up the middle of the state, almost seeming to use I-75 as a guideline to what would cause the most destruction all around. The storm then mashes Miami, flattens Ft. Lauderdale and pulverizes Palm Beach before totally trashing Tampa Bay and then decimating Disney World, demolishing Daytona Beach and tearing through Tallahassee.

By the time the eye of the storm crossed over from what had until now been Florida into Georgia, the leading edge of the storm was chomping big pieces out of Chattanooga. The western borders were just about in Jackson Mississippi and the storm's eastern edges were now milling away in what had until not so long ago been Myrtle Beach South Carolina.

The outpouring devoured everything east of the Mississippi River, all the way back up to what had been the Ohio Valley. The previous full moon surge and the Full Snow Moon on the 14th of February caused each of the great lakes to conjoin, spilling over into the lower states, washing out whole mountain ranges and totally reformatting the entire eastern seaboard. At the North Carolina and Tennessee borders, the storm took a distinctive north easterly turn, putting it on a direct heading with Ottawa, Ontario, Quebec, Nova Scotia Newfoundland and Labrador.

As they enter the Arctic realm, a high-pitched cry signals the end of the celebration. That one shrill voice was followed by a multitude of other voices as the ultra-storm of swirling bubbles spin momentarily on top of the world. The twisting mass tightened its spiral over the Arctic Circle, causing its center to now close tightly.

As the spiraling eye continues to tighten, something even more phenomenal began to happen. The Polar Ice caps were melting and created a warm steam to rise into the evening sky above what had long been the North Pole's polar ice cap. As the polar cap at the top of the earth melts, grown trees and shrubs seem to be forming beneath them and climbing to the surface, much like the Underlings had done.

The largest and final ice cap did not melt away, its warm mist rising into the cool early evening skyline; instead it too began to spin, steadily at first, then faster and faster until it was apparently keeping time with the large snowstorm hovering and rotating directly above it. Once the spinning snow cap evidently matched speeds with the soaring storm above, it appeared to cave in on itself as it dissolved into nothing. The swirling waters once again created a gyrating black hole, but this one didn't spiral upward, it somehow coiled down. The sea was now scrolling downward, into the earth, at its most northern point. The hymn of the Underlings slowly subsided. So did the moisture from the totally melted polar ice caps, as they are literally sucked or vacuumed into the massive spiraling opening. As the waters subside so did the sound of singing, as every underling is seemingly siphoned into it. The immense space continued to drain water from the North Pole, until it became no bigger than a small indentation in the water.

Then it turned into a swirl of bubbles as the twirling vortex sucks in the very last Underling, before entirely closing in on itself, sealing the ditch at the top of the earth. Underlings still celebrated in unison as they wreathed off on their way toward new beginnings. Below the surface, something else extraordinary happened. Sounds of song began again, but at this moment the songs were irritatingly off key. Even this had its purpose, as this was the Underling's manner of regrouping.

Each knew their tribes cry and listened for it as they sang out, a sort of echo location technique, one also used by whales and other sea going mammals. The sound soon became more soothing, as each found its own group and headed off to destinations around the world. The sounds of what was quickly becoming Laila's tribe echoed its way south west, precisely below the earth's surface until it landed on Pico Island in Portugal. There, like molting hot Lava, they spewed out of the top of Alto Peak, a dormant volcano, whose mouth opened some 7,713 feet above sea level, in Mt. Peko Nature Reserve, Pico Island.

It wasn't until they reached this point that Richard had been able to make visual contact with his daughter Laila again. She was now more beautiful than he'd remembered and looked similar to her mother than even he had recollected. But there was something else about her that was different, a variance that Rich just couldn't quite put a finger on. He thought about asking Laila, but immediately decided against it, but still Rich couldn't help but notice her new glow.

Rich no longer considered the fact that he had a job and a pending court date back on the outside. The surface that he now knew had been changed forever. The only thing that mattered any more was his astonishingly beautiful daughter Laila. Even though they had traversed a third of the globe in a day's time they had destroyed it, where mankind is concerned as well.

The fact that he hadn't slept or eaten anything in days had not had the opportunity to sink in, when Laila said to Rich, "Dad, I need to show you something." Rich had no idea what she could possibly want or care to share with him; he also had no intentions of keeping her waiting. No sooner had his long slender fingers touched hers then the two of them were swarming across the Atlantic.

The two myriad northeast toward Ireland and The U.K. and for some reason Rich knew their exact location as far as latitude and longitudes went. It had something to do with the gravitational pull and the temperature of the current against his now thin fluorescent skin. Rich basically set his sights on Plymouth, when at the last minute, Laila made a sharp turn east into the Bay of Biscay, setting them on a direct heading with a well flooded Bordeaux France. Bordeaux nor Pamplona, Barcelona or Marseille had been Laila's objective, which became clear to Rich as soon as she had begun to go in the direction west of Santander Portugal. A few miles west of the washed out beaches of Bordeaux, Laila and Rich descended, nearly half mile in the depth of the inlet. After giving birth, he found any and everything else that life threw at him totally doable as they both soared downward, deep into the cove before once again to the east. They paced themselves deeper, and it got too dark to see, the two of them relied on their own inner light to guide them. Laila lead Richard into what looked like the mouth of a cave way down in the earth, far beneath Bordeaux and its Arcarchon Basin.

Only their own radiance lit the path until the two of them emerged in what Roger could have called an utter miracle. Below the surface of the valley was a virtual roadmap of tubes and tunnels. It was long designed by the underlings to assist them in the world wide task now at hand. The immensity of this below ground cavern is definitely not comparable to anything he had ever remembered seeing in his life. Not even the monstrous size of the chamber paled in comparison to the sight that had met Rich's eyes next. In a somehow brightly lighted section, far beneath France's Basin de' Arcarchon, sat a jumbo 747 transatlantic air craft; Trans-Air flight 143 to Paris France. "What on earth is this place?" Rich questioned in total astonishment.

"You mean what in earth don't you," Laila responded back candidly. "I've never seen one in operation but I'm told that it's a bow wing seven 4T 7" Laila informed her dad proudly. "Well what is it doing down here," he inquired as they both moved nearer to the brightly lit craft. "It was how you say, Plan-B," Laila boasted joyfully, "in case things had gone horribly wrong." As they each got closer, Rich noticed a swarm of workers, canvasing over the jumbo air craft from head to tail and then return again. Works halted temporarily, but only long enough for workers to greet Laila and for her to introduce him and assure them that he was in no way a threat.

Only now were the two of them escorted deep into the airplane, what Rich sees there was even more amazing still. Inside the jumbo aircraft, Rich and Laila see a co-pilot, full staff of flight attendants and 148 travelers. All the commuters and crew members were seat belted firmly into their seats and appeared to be sleeping peacefully; some were heard to snore on occasion. "What had you planned to do with them", he asked, looking back over the almost full cabin of passengers. "Well I couldn't imagine us finding a drive thru to pull into had we needed it to make our escape. So since we didn't have a choice of fast food, I figured they might just have to be our last meal."

Rich had never been on a plane before and was simply amazed at the girth of the monstrosity, as he and Laila are escorted through every section of the plane. In each area of the craft they found more workers, tooling away at either this or that. Not one of the hundreds of workers were Underlings, in fact, they were all surface dwellers, of every nationality, from all over the world. "All working together for the greater good" Laila said smugly to her dad as they entered into a massive though completely empty cargo hold. "Ok," Rich said "I'm impressed, so now that you know you won't need it, what will come of all of this?" "I was thinking we can convert it into a museum," Laila said with what looked like a smirk to Rich through her split top lip.

There were surface dwellers in navy officers uniforms working side by side with what looked to rich like paramedics, hauling things both into and out of the massive air craft. Extra-large pieces were being hauled by an old Ford Falcon wagon pulling a trailer. It had to be as ancient as the car itself, the matching chrome bubble rims on both the worn out automobile and the camper had probably rusted numerous years ago. The driver, looking as if he might have been the Falcon's original owner, worked as hard as everyone else, moving this and that to here and there. Rich had been watching this through one of the plane's many windows and couldn't help but wonder what all of these workers did at break time. As if he actually said it out loud, Laila responded to him, come and I'll show you," she said. As their escort led them back to the aircraft's loading bay. The two of them parted company from the tall attractive attendant. Rich sensed a strong urge to express gratitude for their closely guarded tour. As Rich turned to say thank you, he instantly noticed the boyish good looks and the name tag on the breast pocket of the uniform of their handsome guide; J. Striker.

From the plane, Laila took Rich to another brilliant spot in the cave deep beneath Bordeaux and its Arcarchon Basin. For the first time since leaving the Anchor Bar, Rich can now hear music, coming from the brightly lit area just ahead of them. They rounded the corner when Rich and Laila came face to face with the proprietors of Earl's Buckhead Bar B Que.

The cause of the brilliant glow they had been able to see, even from the plane, was now right before both their eyes. The biggest rotating slow cooker Rich had ever seen loaded as high up as he could visualize. There were slabs of ribs, shoulders and rump that he was pretty sure was not pork. "Welcome to Earls, boys and girls, best darned bar-b-que in the underworld. If yawl good folks are ready to eat then my wife Irene will lead yawl both to a good seat. "But neither of them had been there to take or to partake, only to observe. "Does this help to answer your question," Laila asked as Rich now surveyed all that was around and before them. "That helped to remedy that particular question," Rich pondered to himself, but it had only caused more questions to rain on his brain. "How on earth did you find out about this place," he thought without saying, staring at her face, hoping for some facial expression that would never come. "This has nothing to do with me finding out Dad, it's about what I feel I must now do with the information that I have.

"Laila turned toward Rich and looked him straight in the eyes and relayed this message to him. "I didn't create the mess that I've found here, so I have two choices, either I fix it or live with it." "You created me into this unrest; I didn't choose to be born into it. Although I'm here, I have no desire to die in it Dad. I know that I can make a difference, together we can make a difference." Rich suddenly filled with pride, at the same time he felt scared to death.

Your blood made me smart, Namow's blood made me strong, my desire made me queen, and my strength will make me an unstoppable force." She turned away from rich, bowed her head and assured him. "Together you and I can repopulate the planet with a new species, the most powerful monarch on earth, but either you'll have to help me kill Namow or she'll help me kill you.

Rich had thought her comment humorous, for about the first twenty seconds, until he'd read her eyes. Laila was dead serious, Rich saw it, but he didn't dare think he should let her know that he had seen it. With no hesitation Laila continued on. "We don't have another major swarm until the next full moon. We've got a lot to get done by then, so if you follow me I'd like to continue to tour now," Laila says as she leads rich further into the enormous cave structure. In passing, the two of them came upon six ambulances, in an even smaller cavern. "Are you preparing for a major medical emergency?" Rich asked concernedly. "They came cheap," Laila said without changing her expression in the least bit. "Are you ready for the piece de resistance?" Laila asked as she neared the base of a tube, the Underling's idea of an elevator.

"You do remember how this works, don't you?" she said, as she slithers into the tube. Rich did not help but wonder what Laila had meant by that, Laila couldn't help but read his thoughts. "How long did Namow keep you enslaved in that hole before you realized you were able to escape?" Laila asked.

"Had she not knocked you up, you might still be down there, or even worse, dinner by now." Rich followed her into the tube and up, seemingly to the end of the earth before a sharp turn lead them both into the largest space Rich had seen yet.

Rich actually rubbed his eyes to see if he was really seeing what it was that was here before his eyes. This couldn't be real he thought, because he was now looking at an area filled with every breed of animal, bug and rodent known to man, "And a few not known to mankind," Laila said, again with a straight face. "Are they all going to be food for workers as well?" Rich glanced in Laila's direction.

"You're sense of humor is so humanly old fashioned dad," Laila said as she now hovered mere inches from Rich and looked into his eyes. "What gives humans the right to kill and digest animals smarter than themselves, not to fill a hunger, but a thirst?" Rich wasn't sure exactly where she had gotten her information from, but he also knew that he would not have to ask. Acinonyx jubatus, a large feline from the family Felidae, subfamily Felinae or cat, inhabited most of Africa and parts of the Middle East, the only extant member of the genus Acinonyx. It can run faster than any other land animal, as fast as 112 to 120 km per hour or 70 to 75 mph in short bursts, covering distances up to 500 meters or 1,600 ft., it has the ability to accelerate from 0 to 100 km or 62 mph in three seconds. Although notable for modifications in the species' paws the cheetah is one of the few felids with semi-retractable claws.

"Your kind can't out run them, can't out fight them and can't camouflage yourself to hide from the likes of them. Just the same you feel you have the right to kill them and for what, their skins?" "The whale and the elephant are both the largest mammals on earth that lived harmoniously in deep woods and in the cavernous seas, yet man found a way to encroach upon their habitats as well and take their lives, for sport. Certainly my intentions are to replenish the earth's population, with every type known to mankind, except one."

Rich thought for sure that with so many animals, of innumerable different species in the same location that the noise would be deafening.

But excluding his communications with Laila, there was total silence. "You see what I mean?" Laila tuned in, "you pay so much attention to what your thoughts say and desire, yet so little to what your senses suppose you need." Richard placed both his hands to the sides of his head, "Only now do you realize you don't require ears to hear what is necessary to be heard," Laila explained.

"Is the goal to wipe all living souls off of the face of the earth all together?" he inquired. "That would be like mass genocide, humans are already infamously known for that. I would not care to be remembered for such treachery. Besides, if we were to render individuals extinct, who would do all the hard labor and the maintenance?" Laila asked in all honesty.

Rich looked at Laila now with total astonishment. He couldn't believe either that a child he brought into this world can be so hideously ruthless, or because he was still in shock of the reality that he no longer had ears.

"I realize how difficult it must be for you to wrap your head around the idea that your beautiful baby girl could be so cruel, but that's ok, I'm still trying to wrap my head around the fact that I was born to a father who until at this moment has not realized he has no ears." " Well I guess you've got it all figured out how you intend to house and feed the amount of people it's going to take for you to pull off this whatever it is you think you're doing?" Rich glared at her in disgust. "Of course I do old man," Laila vocalized. "So you had best cool your jets. Come on, I'm part you aren't I. That means I too have an extreme case of OCD, meaning I too am prone to serious cases of the persnicketies, and I want everything precise, does any of that sound familiar at all to you? Daddy"

Rich had never thought that someday his faults might literally come back to bite him in the ass. But in his current situation there seemed to be a fine chance of that happening. "Come with me Dad," Laila signaled to him. "I have got something else to show you, just to reassure you that all is not yet lost." He couldn't help but wonder which hole in the earth she had stored it in. "On the contrary my good man, and because I know you're old, I'm going to warn you, we're headed to the Philippine Sea."

"The Philippines are a few thousand miles on the other side of the planet" he uttered. "9,621 nautical miles," Laila answered, "but I know a short cut we can take, kind of as the crow flies." Having the gut feeling that his options were extremely limited, Rich agreed to come along on the trip. Within moments of the two of them arriving back at the main mouth of the cave, she turned to him yet again. "Are you sure you're up for another long excursion so soon, I mean you're ancient, you probably need rest," Laila stated disrespectfully. "I'm certain the tread won't be as hard on me as you might think. Give your old dad a little credit," Rich said as both paused momentarily at the opening of the giant cavern. "Swim," Laila yelled to him, "Time permitting, I hadn't intended on you swimming all that distance. Without warning, Laila screamed out into the darkness of the deep sea. The sound of her echo penetrated the depth, seemingly only to get lost in the ocean's quiet vastness. In a very short instant the water almost seemed to boil with all kinds of sea creatures, from the minutest minnow, to the massive man eaters. He did not question the reason she had called so many species of sea life to assemble here at this moment. Then she totally mutated, to what looked to Rich like one of the fattest and ugliest eels he'd ever seen.

Rich didn't even have time to react. He was then sucked up in a fail swoop by the massive mouth of the beast that he just watched his daughter turn into and then devoured whole. This being done, Laila set forth across the sea, her Entourage of sea creatures following her in close tow.

By the time Laila arrived in Palawan, Manamoc Islands in the Philippines, the sorted swarms of meat seekers had all sauntered off course in search of something edible. She literally washed up on shore and vomited up her entire inner contents within moments of arriving. As Rich poured out of her stomach and onto the beach, Laila reformed to Laila as Rich once again became an earless Halfling. A deserted Island was the first thing that had come to mind as he surveyed their new surroundings. "Once upon a time," replied Laila, "I didn't like the décor, so I've made some changes here and there, please, allow me to show you around."

Had Rich still possessed a nose he would have immediately detected the rank, god-awful smell of rotting meat and feces. A short distance from the beach, Rich saw exactly what was causing the decaying odor. In a field that spread as far as the eye could see, were humans, standing shoulder to shoulder, no room to lie or even sit. Hundreds of people, their faces unusually bloated, their bellies distended.

Each and every one showed signs of severe diabetic edema. Some had legs and feet so swollen that the skin actually ruptured, spawning pus to drip from their open and infected wounds, into the urine and excrement soaked earth. The dead and dying are trampled beneath the feet of those still healthy enough to maintain their balance. Mouths hung open on faces contorted from horror, devastation and defeat. Rich could not hear, but he was sure he sensed them crying out to their God and maker to have mercy on them. Day after day, they watch as tens of others around them are picked out for that day's slaughter. People too sick and too bloated to defend themselves where they stood, none the less run, were snatched from the herd each day by their arms, legs, hair, even crowns. The others looked on as each are hovered upside down and beheaded. Their torsos are left hanging until sunset to assure full drainage of its blood. The heads are immediately skewered with long sticks and submerged in large vats of human body fat until night fall. Then they are used as torches to illuminate the outer edges of their confinement. Each figure is then carefully disemboweled, their warm, still beating heart a special treat for the one that gets the honor of doing the gutting.

With this being done, not one of them are removed from the coils that bind them at the ankles. Instead they are all taken down together. Their bodies are then dragged to the beach, where it's washed and soaked in ocean water until the meat is pale and tender to the touch. Only then are the prime pieces separated and stored for not so future use.

The larger chunks are heated until the oils are extracted. Then the flesh and bone are finely ground together to make a thick pasty pudding that is in turn served to the massive number of herded humans still awaiting their chance to hang and be drained. Some males were actually lifted out of their confines, had their testicles and penis torn from between their thighs and were then thrown back amongst the others in their confinement. Their screams tormented only their own ears, as they cry to a God that seems to have given up on getting them out of yet another predicament.

As they unknowingly cannibalize their own dead, men are forced to do strenuous manual labor. While heavier women were first heated for their oils and then either boiled into a broth or ground into a thick grub. Thinner ladies were skinned alive and dissected for research. Some of the luckier ones are actually kept as favorites; literally hog-tied around the neck by their owner underling and treated like prized pets.

Rich remembered back over all the times that he had chowed down on a burger or chicken leg, without giving it any more thought than he might have, had he bitten a banana. "I think we should let you get your rest now Dad, you're beginning to look a little green around the gills if I should say so myself, no pun intended." "I'd probably hate to see what you do for fun and recreation," he said, surveying his surroundings.

"Well, let's find out," Laila challenged him. I'm sure the things that pass for recreation and sport with us isn't much different than what passes for amusement or pastime with the surface dwellers." "Give me your hand Dad", Laila said with a smile that told Rich he had no choice but to reach out to her. Instantly, she and Rich are telepathically transported to the African Plains, where a mother cheetah was about to take down a gazelle that she had chased for many kilometers, in an attempt to keep itself and its two young cubs from starving. Seconds before she made contact, she is dropped by a hunter's bullet. Her muscular body skinned and left to the hyena and other scavengers leaving her offspring, not old enough to fend for themselves. The pups are then ripped apart by marauders or sold into captivity, to be shown off at the local zoo.

A bull elephant quietly grazes in the trees with its family. No known predators are in its native jungle habitat. Suddenly a loud sound shatters the silence. The leader of the pack lies dead. A hole put through its head with its body left to rot after its massive ivory horns are sheared off, same with the wide toed ungulates you call rhinoceros. Great whales of the deep are slaughtered at the surface for small amounts of ivory, not for food, but for what? Just to decorate your own ugly figures with jewelry. Minks, ferrets, raccoons, eel, rabbit, fox even mole are skinned alive so that their bodies' natural protectant can enhance your own flesh. A Giraffe's hide is used to adorn your feet; what makes you worthy?"

"Your species take pearls and shark's teeth to make trinkets to embellish your skin. You pilfer alabaster and onyx, diamonds, gold, copper and steel, even salt you steal from the soil. What you fail to realize is, all of these things are present where they are for a reason, and thus they were put there for a purpose. Nature has a very fine balance on earth and everything is where it is for justification. When you extracted over 200 metric tons of gold from the ground over your years of reign here, did you know that the gold in the dirt is what balances the globe with the sun, keeping us in perfect celestial alignment in our solar system?

Did you know that the rocks that you call diamonds were once only lumps of coal, pushed up from earth's mantle through its inner core, to its outer core? This is how the land maintains its warmth. Gems in large quantities, store radiation that helps to heat the planet, but your kind sees it only as a pretty stone that you can possess. When you pull oils and gasses from deep within the turf, what do you think replaces the void that you leave there?"

"Of course you've never given it much thought. You've never given much thought to why the terra has been made high in some places and low in others. Your only thoughts about stars in the sky have been about how you might profit from them or how you are going to protect yourself from others that might come from them."

"You slaughter birds yet you've not mastered flight, you kill fish yet you can't breathe under water." "Your people dam rivers, blocking their flow to the sea, for your own selfish means. Yet, if your own breed is a different shade in color than you are, then they too become a threat to you. They turn into enemies that are feared, loathed and killed so that you might feel safe in the confines of your sanctuary you have created. Dead things that you have amassed are simply there to show others around you that you are living."

"Every insect on the planet has a reason and a design, Vultures, hyena and even the lowly maggot has purpose, to devour the dying, decaying and rotting filth. What is your intention here on earth dad? You could let go of my hand now too" Laila said. As soon as he did, the two of them were back standing on that beach in the Philippians once again. "So is this all just some kind of vendetta against humans, or as you so fondly call us, Surface Dwellers?" Rich asked her now from deep in thought. "Not at all Daddy," Laila said. "This is a race for the species, and I bet you can easily guess which one is losing."

"The sun will go down soon; it's time to set the torches around the edges of the compound. For some reason it seems to sooth them, as they still appear to fear the night and the things that lurk there in. Shall I have them prepare a berth for you Father?" Laila inquired of Rich. "Looks to be fitting given that we do come across to be on somewhat of a world cruise. I'm certain you've heard of the land of milk and honey, haven't you Dad? because I have."

"Sure I have Richard responded back, what about it?"

"This isn't it" Laila said, vibrating all over in brilliant shades of fluorescence. "Aw come on Dad, didn't you think that at all funny?" "You've got a warped sense of humor," Rich answered honestly. "I get it from my Momma" replied Laila. "But I wanna grow up to be exactly like you; let's go now," Laila persuades, "We're burning daylight."

They approached what Rich could only describe as a massive tar pit, with thousands of spikes stuck out all around its edges. Laila started to shine even brighter now as they neared the first staff. He reached out toward the nearest stick and Laila smacked his hand with such force that they both saw sparks.

"That's called Manual Labor for a Reason Father, as you're no longer the man you were." This being said, Laila let out a bellowing scream that reverberated like a shock wave across the shore. Within seconds, from all around the beach, they came out of the darkness like walking zombies. Men, their faces once filled with desperation, now infused with despair, scuttled out of the shadows, one by one arriving at the tar pit to claim a stick. The first man to grab his branch broke into an almost catatonic state. He himself was required to come to Laila to get fire, which he would then share with all of the others.

The man all but crawled over to where Laila waited with Rich near the edge of the large tar pit. He slowly lifted his stick with the human head soaked in body grease near Laila and Rich, though never daring to lift his eyes up to either of them. Laila pointed a thin digit toward the saturated skull, and then began to hum. The glow from her figure seemed to pour into her arm and out of her finger as the oil drenched crown burst into a brilliant blue flame.

Head still bowed, the man squirmed backwards for the first ten or so yards before turning and scampering back to the edge of the woods. There the one small light soon became two, then twenty, then two hundred, as it continued to spread from staked head to staked head, around the island. "This is one chore that I would love to assign to an underling, no pun intended," Laila relayed. "There are just so many more important things that I could be doing then being out here playing the fire goddess for a bunch of zombie living mufuckers." "Do you kiss your mother with that mouth?" Richard asked sarcastically. "Actually, I ate my mother with this mouth," Laila reverberated back quickly.

Rich thought for sure that what he had just heard must indeed have been a joke. Laila had apparently learned an awful lot in her long four days of life. He was pretty confident that lying was not one of the traits that she had picked up. "Speaking of Namow, where is she anyway? I've not seen her in a while."

"Did you not hear what I just said Daddy, I ate Mom." Rich stared at her, as he wondered if she actually meant what she was saying. "You see Dad, in life you have to be aware of the rules, how else can you play by them?" "You see, there are these things called domains and dynasties and they are all headed by kings and or queens, even ants know that and live by it. Every community, no matter how large, only has one queen. Momma proclaimed to me that she was and would always be the leading light of our colony Dad. Long did she reign. But since there should be only one ruler to a district, that bitch had to go, so I devoured her. There's no denying that. The question now dad, is whether the new monarch will sit on the throne over her current commune with or without a king. That part I am leaving up to you dear Daddy. Wasn't that nice of me, entrusting such a huge decision to my beloved old Dad?"

"Now we gather for the feast of plenty," Laila said looking directly at Rich, and Daddy, you're my guest of honor." "I can hardly wait," Rich replied quickly. "You'll hardly have to she responded," seconds before touching his hand, transporting them both back to the beach front, where greasy head torches, lined up along the beach, now lit what looked to Rich like a Hawaiian Luau. There were no dancers dressed in palm skirts, shearing flower leis. At the center of the lighted track was a massively large ditch.

At intervals around the outer edges of the massive pit were smaller pits, all with long skewers, each loaded from end to end with meat.

At first glance, it looked too Rich as though three baby pigs were skewered on each, until he took a closer look. He was instantly sick to his stomach and felt the need to throw up. He then realized that the last time he had thrown up was when he gave birth to Laila. Rich tried desperately to think of anything but the view before him; Laila had every intention of making that close to impossible. "I'm not very hungry," Rich said. "But you're the guest of honor," Laila replied. "I'm 3rd generation vegan," Rich echoed back quickly, to which Laila responded, "Then out of respect I'll only have you carve," Laila echoed back. "I'd rather not," Rich said. "It's still flesh, not even Kosher." "And you're not even Jewish," Laila echoed back. Her whole body now shivered in neon glow. "OK, here's the deal Daddy-O, everyone in this tribe pulls their weight. We don't have quote unquote nine to five jobs with pensions and 401Ks, but we do have a sense of order here that works well for us thus far."

Rich was still looking away, but he was nonetheless anticipating what he knew was yet to come. "So you don't want to be my meat carver, because being a vegetarian you just can't bring yourself to handle strange meat. Well what about this offer Dad," Laila corresponded. "Manage your own sustenance dad, and together you and I could repopulate the earth." Rich turned to leave and immediately Laila was there before him again. "What's wrong with me? Am I not attractive enough? I can be whatever your heart desires, blond brunette, redhead, hair down to my ass or a bald heifer, whatever you want." Laila spread out on the massive rocks at the water's edge, posing for Rich, as if to show him each and all of her sexy sides.

Rich turned away once more and again he found Laila within inches of his face, staring directly into his eyes. "Look at me dam you, look at me, you know you want me. How can you not, you created me out of great pleasure and now dam it, and you're going to love me." Rich looked elsewhere yet again, but this time Laila wasn't having it. She reached for rich yet again, this time her long fingers scissoring forward, her talon like nails ripping painfully through Rich's thin skin.

Before he even realized what had occurred, Rich reacted, but not with his hands, with his mouth. What happened had taken place so quickly that it caught Rich totally off guard as well. Both his upper and lower jaw, instantly unhinged from his face. It catapulted out close to four feet, to lock on Laila's face tearing it from her skull in one quick swipe. She didn't even have the chance to defend herself. Her face was now gone completely. Laila swiped violently at the air in front of her, as if anticipating her attacker to lunge ahead to finish her off. But Rich, not being sure what was going on himself, felt almost as if he were watching from afar. The teeth that had just launched themselves from his feature, ravished what had for a short time been his only child, from the top to bottom.

The teeth didn't stop swirling around what had been Laila until there was nothing left. Not even a wet spot in the sand to show that she had been there only moments before.

Rich stood, momentarily flabbergasted and in total awe as the incisors that had just ejected themselves from his own mouth, rose up and hovered in front of him briefly. There seemed to be items that were ingested regurgitating from between the denticle, pouring first downward toward the sand, then up to fill the void above the still chattering teeth. He thought for sure as he watched the body reform that he was about to be faced with the wrath of Laila. Instead the face that formed around the opening wasn't that of Laila, but Namow.

Rich wasn't positive what had just happened, but the consequences of his actions were greatly appreciated. "Namow, what the, where did, how did . . . ?" "I never intended to leave you here alone Rich," she stated. "The evil that you and I created literally consumed me," Namow said. "I got you involved in all of this Rich; I couldn't just go away and let you fend for yourself after it was me that started all of this mess." "It was my foolish idea to create life with you; it was also on me to protect you from the ramifications." "But Laila mentioned that she had eaten you," he responded. "Yeah, she did, that ungrateful little bitch, but what she failed to realize when I gave her little horny ass life was that, I too reserve the right to take it from her."

Rich didn't care what her reasoning was; he only knew that more than anything he'd wanted to give her a big hug right now. "Namow, how, or what just happened," he flourished. "If I had to guess, I'd say that I probably just saved your life, again and you're welcome," answered Namow.

"I would cuddle you but, it seems that every time you and I connect, something weird always happens" said Rich. "What if I promised not to eat you or impregnate you?" replied Namow. Her arms now stretched out to accept his hug. Slowly he moved closer to her until the both merged in vibrant color. Their embrace seemed to last for ages, as the sun was already coming up over the eastern portion of the island. "But what about Laila, is she . . . ?" "Laila was only a trial run, and trial runs are prone to recalls," Namow replied with a flash. "You came back though Namow, so did I, so will Laila be coming back as well?" Rich asked. "I'm sure she will" said Namow. "But please don't tell me that you're also afraid of a little fertilizer. Rich dimmed in brightness just a bit as he looked directly into the greenest eyes he had ever seen. "So where do we go from here," he questioned, the two still holding each other close. 'Well if you're asking me, to sleep, I could use a nap.

As they lay down together by the light of the almost full Worm Moon, Namow and Rich nuzzled against each other softly, as gently as the waves now caressed the shore line.

"Shouldn't we be celebrating the eve of the full pink moon and preparing for tomorrow's full pink moon ceremony right now Namow," Rich asked. "It's the final stage, the grand finale, the end of the world." "Or the beginning," said Namow, "you've shown me a lot about humanity that I never knew before. Things I wish I had known before now." The two cuddled closely atop a sand dune. She held Rich close and caressed his face until he dozed off.

Rich was enjoying the sensation of the warm hands caressing his face and felt himself drifting into what he referred to as dream consciousness. The caress became less soothing as Rich could feel himself now actually being awakened from what apparently had become an intense sleep. "Rich, if you can hear me, open your eyes," the voice said. This voice was far too deep to have been Namow and Rich's eyes sprang open suddenly. Rich once again found himself staring into the most beautiful blue eyes he had ever seen, but it wasn't her who's face he now stared into. The emblem on the blue jacket that the woman wore told Rich instantly that she was a Paramedic. The smell and the old faded yellow tiles on the wall let him know that he is in the bathroom of the Rusty Anchor. The heads that were popping up surrounding all the pretty paramedics were familiar to him. Around him and behind the medics stood Adam Gray, Carl McNeal, Danny Skip turner, Giovanni Pirelli, Theodore Grimsby and Sidney Sye Greenburg," all looking drunk yet highly concerned about him.

"I guess after that knock on the head you really shouldn't have been drinking is what we're thinking both Adam and Carl said, almost in unison. Rich tried to sit up, but the paramedic pressed her palm gently into his chest, demanding that he not yet move. As the guys helped the two female paramedics to get Rich first onto a back board and then onto the stretcher, the shorter one said to Rich, "Just lay back, relax and enjoy the ride Rich, you're in good hands, I promise you. Rich couldn't help but notice the small scar in the center of her top lip.

This book is dedicated to the best woman in the world. She has been by my side through the editing process. I love Judy dearly. To my parents and siblings, my daughters and my new grandson who I hope follow in my footsteps.